The Fifth Di
August 2024

Novelette
25   The Ascent of Old Cormac 'Round the Horn of the Moon by Lawrence Buentello

Short Stories
6   The Children of Summer by Kellee Kranendonk
60   The Alchemist and Her House by Anj Baker
74   Slumber in the Garden by Mason Wageman

Flash Fiction
57   The Lotus Seller by S. Cameron David

Poetry
21   Clockwise Dreams by Holly Day
24   Subject: After Death by Debby Feo
53   Taurus Season by Hillary Smith-Maddern
56   A Place and a Thing by Holly Day
59   Pages of Waste by Holly Day
72   The Lowing of the Stars at Night by Holly Day
73   Lasting Legacy by Lauren McBride
92   Apparently Most Serial Killers are Virgos by Hillary Smith-Maddern

93   Who's Who

THE STAFF OF THE FIFTH DI...:

EDITOR: Tyree Campbell
WEBMASTER: H David Blalock
COVER DESIGNERS: Laura Givens; Marcia A. Borell

Cover art "Cocooning World" by Teri & Nic Santitoro
Cover design by Laura Givens

Vol. V, No.2   August 2024

The Fifth Di... is published three times a year on the 1st day of April, August, and December in the United States of America by Hiraeth Publishing, P.O. Box 1248, Tularosa, NM, 88352. Copyright 2024 by Hiraeth Publishing. All rights revert to authors and artists upon publication except as noted in selected individual contracts. Nothing may be reproduced in whole or in part without written permission from the authors and artists. Any similarity between places and persons mentioned in the fiction or semi-fiction and real places or persons living or dead is coincidental. Writers and artists guidelines are available online at www.hiraethsffh.com. Guidelines are also available upon request from Hiraeth Publishing, P.O. Box 1248, Tularosa, NM, 88352, if request is accompanied by a self-addressed #10 envelope with a first-class US stamp. Editor: Tyree Campbell.

A Little Help, Please

In the world of the small indie press we fight a never-ending battle for attention to our work, as writers and in publishing. Here's an example: big publishers [you know who they are] have gobs of $$$ that they can devote to advertising and marketing. Here at Hiraeth Publishing, our advertising budget consists of the deposits for whatever soda bottles and aluminum cans we can find alongside the highways. Anti-littering laws make our task even more difficult . . . ☺

That's where YOU come in. YOU are our best promoter. YOU are the one who can tell others about us. Just send 'em to our website, tell them about our store. That's all. Just that.

Of course, we don't mind if you talk us up. We're pretty good, you know. We have some award-winning and award-nominated writers and artists, plus other voices well-deserving to be heard [not everyone wins awards, right?] but our publications are read-worthy nevertheless.

That number once again is:
www.hiraethsffh.com

Friend us on Facebook at Hiraeth Publishing
Follow us on Twitter at @HiraethPublish1

Pevely Keiser in:
THE IPHAJEAN LARK

Five hundred years into the future, Pevely Keiser is the capo of the criminal organization called Temmen. Temmen runs itself, for the most part, with only a few nudges from Pevely to keep people in line. Lately she has two things on her mind. She wants to do something good and useful with the funds that accrue to the gang. And she wants a companion or two to help her…and perhaps to share her bed, for she well knows it's lonely at the top.

In the process of training her two new assistants (and possible companions) Pevely comes across a young woman being chased. Taking her on board, Pevely soon learns of a devastating conspiracy that threatens the Confederation with totalitarian rule. The key to the solution lies in the hands of one of her employees, but is it the right key? Only the corporate hierarch who leads the conspiracy knows for sure. And he is the father of the woman Pevely rescued.

https://www.hiraethsffh.com/product-page/iphajean-lark-by-tyree-campbell

The Children of Summer
Kellee Kranendonk

Tires crunched on the snow as Meghan pulled her car to a stop. "I think we're lost, Shaune," she said to her friend and passenger.

"I told you I was bad at reading these things." Shaune folded the paper map, ignoring the creases that were already there. "But it *is* beautiful here."

Both women sat quietly looking at the snow-covered scene. A modest brick church sat on the side of the dead-end road, an apple orchard to its left. Gnarled trees, some with frozen, rust-coloured fruit still hanging from leafless limbs, wore white blankets from yesterday's storm. The bright sun turned the covering into blinding diamonds.

A snow-covered winged angel sat atop a brick bell tower rising up from the back of the church. His arms were curled on his chest and his head drooped to one side. Smaller angels in the same pose decorated a wooden deck at the front of the church. Ornately carved wooden posts supported it.

Up ahead, where the road ended was a small graveyard; perhaps a dozen black and grey stones poked up through the white layer. A wrought iron sign that had seen better days read 'Saint Peter's Cemetery'.

"Kinda creepy though," Shaune said softly.

"Yeah. It's almost like time forgot this place." It was more of a feeling than an observance. There had only been a low-slung building housing a post office and a convenience store, and two homes. The parking lot to the building had not been plowed. In an empty, snow-covered field behind one of the homes, about a half dozen children played.

Shaune pointed. "Maybe there's someone in that church that can help. At least the parking lot's cleared."

Then it occurred to Meghan. "Now *that* is really weird," she said. "This old country road is plowed and the church lot, but not the one for the store and post office?"

"Today is Saturday, isn't it?" asked Shaune.

"Yeah," agreed Meghan. That might make sense for the post office, but what about the store and the church?

As if reading her mind, Shaune said, "Maybe they're Seventh Day Adventists?"

"Wouldn't the kids be in church too then?"

The women looked at one another, neither having an answer.

"The pastor might have to do something on a Saturday?" offered Shaune.

"Maybe." Meghan nodded. But then a shiver ran down her spine despite the heat in the car. A knot formed in her gut. "I don't want to go in there." She reached to put the car in reverse when her friend grabbed her arm.

"Wait!" Shaune pointed again. "Look, there's an old man coming out of the church. Maybe he can help."

The old man had spied them there and, as he watched, Meghan sensed his judgement coming down on them, radiating from eyes that stared out from beneath a grey tuque. His heavy coat hung on his skinny frame and pants tucked into his boots gave him a sort of comical clownish look. The knot tightened.

Meghan sighed and climbed out of the car. Icy air hit her warm face. She was glad of no wind. "Shaune, I have a bad feeling about this. And I'm *not* quoting Star Wars."

Shaune didn't reply as they headed toward the little church.

"You girls lost?"

"Actually we are," said Shaune. "Wonder if you could help us?"

"Mayhap. Come inside where it's warm and I'll see what I can do."

The women exchanged glances. Shaune shrugged. Meghan glanced at the support posts as she climbed the stairs. Each one was the same, depicting Adam and Eve lolling in Eden along with several animals, birds and fish. No snakes or insects of any sort.

Inside wasn't as warm as the car, but it *was* warmer than outside. Meghan blinked against the dark interior. Deep brown panelling covered the walls. Wooden pews had been stained the same deep brown. Even the carpeting was dark brown.

The blonde wood pastor's dais, the white choir chairs, and a gold painted crucifix hanging on the wall stood out in the gloom. A hymn number board, and stained-glass windows, were the only other things decorating the walls.

The patterned windows of red, blue, yellow, purple and white muted the daylight coming in, though dust motes danced in lightly coloured beams of sun. Each of four panels depicted a different scene: infant Jesus in his mother's arms, a female Meghan guessed was Mary Magdalene, Jesus on the cross, and the last showed a tomb in front of a sunrise.

"There's some leftover food in the fridge," offered the old man, "and I can put on a pot of coffee."

"We're not that lost," said Meghan. She just wanted to get out of here. It wasn't that she couldn't remember the last time she was in a church, but this place creeped her out more than any of the ethereal figures she'd seen this past summer in the graveyards she'd visited.

"Well, what are you looking for?" The old guy took off his hat. The wisps of white hair he had left stood up in two staticky horns. Shaune clamped her hand over her mouth to stifle a giggle. The old guy didn't seem to notice.

"We're going to a friend's baby shower," Meghan said. "She's moved into a new house and neither of us has been there before. I guess we took a wrong turn."

He nodded. "Happens. Where does this friend live?"

Shaune jumped in. "She said Saint Peter. We saw the cemetery sign, but I don't think this is the right place."

The old guy nodded again and held up two fingers. "There are two Saint Peters. This is the old Saint Peter. You probably want the new one."

Turning away from them, the old guy muttered something then started hobbling away.

Shaune turned to Meghan. "What's he doing?"

Meghan shrugged. "I have no idea. Come on, let's get out of here."

"Maybe we should wait a minute."

"For what?"

Shaune sat in a pew. "Maybe," she said, "he's going to get a map to show us the difference between the two places."

"We have a map!" Then Meghan muttered, "For all the good it did us."

"Can we just wait and see if he comes back?"

"I think you're crazy, but okay, fine!" Meghan gaze around the church. Shadows in the dark corners seemed to writhe up and down the walls, and a light mist appeared to rise from the choir chairs. Turning back to Shaune, Meghan found her friend engrossed in a hymnal. "Shaune," she hissed.

Shaune looked up.

At the same time, a tall, slender man wearing black dress pants and a white shirt hurried out of the door the old man had gone through. He had a black robe slung over his arm and keys in his hand. He startled when he saw them. "Oh, I didn't know anyone was here."

"What about that other guy?" asked Meghan. More than just confusion was tugging at her knots.

The man frowned. "I'm the only one here. Or I thought I was. Can I help you girls?"

"We're looking for a friend's place. She lives in St. Peter," blurted Shaune. "The new one, according to the old man."

The guy shook his head. "There's no old man here but me. But I see the problem. This used to be Saint Peter, but it's now called Saint Pierre." He held up his hand as Shaune opened her mouth to speak. "No one ever bothered to change the name on the graveyard sign. This all happened when some wise-guy politician decided to split Saint Peter into two towns. Rather than East and West Saint Peter, we ended up with a Saint Peter and a Saint Pierre." He smiled. There was something not quite right about it, something disconcerting that Meghan couldn't quite put her finger on. "People confuse them all the time. Even the locals."

"Oh." Meghan had no idea what else to say. Why hadn't the other guy said that? And why didn't this guy seem to know about him?

"Well, I guess we best be getting along now," he said, without offering them any more help.

The girls followed him back to the door, Meghan thinking about checking the map herself – surely Shaune wasn't that bad at reading towns on a map - then backtracking to the last road sign they'd seen.

The man pulled the door open only to find snow piled as high as his waist, and a blizzard so violent that the girls couldn't see their car across the street. The wind screamed like someone in distress as it flung clusters of snow onto the church's occupants.

"Oh my God," shouted Meghan.

"It was sunny out there when we came in," cried Shaune.

The man pushed the door against the gale. Getting it closed, he leaned against it and wiped his forehead with his arm. "I guess we're not going anywhere."

Meghan's sense of dread deepened. Come on, Meg, she thought. He's just a man. What can he do against two women?

"There are refreshments in the kitchen," he said, pointing to a wide set of stairs leading to what Meghan presumed to be the basement. "You girls go on ahead. I'm going to make a phone call and I'll join you when I finish."

The girls watched him walk back up the aisle. Meghan leaned in to whisper in Shaune's ear. "Do you feel that?"

"Feel what?"

"I don't know." Meghan shrugged. "It's like... something... I don't know. Just a strange feeling. Like maybe something is off."

Shaune nodded. "Yeah, something's weird about this place. What happened to that other guy?"

Sighing, Meghan shook her head. "I don't know." So *it's not just me, I'm not imagining things.*

Shaune put her hands on her hips. "But really, how can it be snowing that hard?"

"I don't know that either. I guess it can't hurt to have a cup of coffee though. Maybe the storm will be over when we're done." The feeling in her gut, and the beat of her heart were at odds with her words. But right now she had no idea what else to do.

"Are we going down there?" Shaune pointed to the stairs, appeared to be debating what to do. "Well, I guess there's nothing else to do," she responded to her own question.

Tables draped in white cloth, like ghostly furniture in an abandoned house filled the darkened basement. At the bottom of the stairs, on the right, was a light switch. Meghan flipped it. Only half the lights went on.

"Oh, that's just creepy!"

"No kidding." Meghan looked around. The lights had only partially dispelled the darkness, leaving shadows in the rest of the room. The same dark panelling made up the walls down here and there were no windows. Signs on the two doors to the left proclaimed the rooms to be 'Junior Sunday School' and 'Senior Sunday School'.

"Where's the kitchen?" asked Shaune.

A quick search revealed a hallway next to the stairs leading to a small kitchen. Another switch, installed upside down, turned on a flickering fluorescent light.

"Nope," said Meghan and flipped the switch off again.

"Maybe it'll stop," argued Shaune and turned the light on again. "It's too dark to see anything."

"I'm blaming you if I get a migraine." Meghan spotted the coffee maker and went to fill it with water. The faucet sputtered air and spit gobs of dirty water. When it finally ran smooth, slimy red ooze poured out. "Oh my God, Shaune!" She dropped the kettle on the floor.

At the same time, Shaune screamed and slammed the fridge door. They turned to one another, both screaming, "What was that?"

Meghan leaned against the door frame, pinching the bridge of her nose between her finger and thumb. She closed her eyes against the strobing light. Her heart beat like a drum, adrenaline prickling through her veins. "Breathe, just breathe. Shaune, what happened?"

"There was a hand in the fridge."

"A hand?"

"Yeah, what were you screaming about?"

Meghan looked at the faucet, now running with clear, clean water. "Never mind." It must have been rust, she told herself as she pushed away from the doorframe. At the fridge she grasped the handle. With a glance toward Shaune, she opened it.

Her heart stopped, leapt into her throat. There *was* a hand in there. But she noticed something odd about it as Shaune came up behind her.

Meghan reached in. Shaune screamed at her not to touch it. Meghan picked up the plate the hand was lying on. Turning to her friend, she drew her finger across it, pink flesh gathering on her fingertip.

"What are you doing?" Shaune's face had gone pasty white.

Meghan inserted her finger into her mouth. Shaune clamped both hands over her mouth, her eyes stretched wide. For the first time since entering this place, Meghan felt the urge to giggle. "It's cake, Shaune." Breaking into laughter, she spewed cake and frosting into the air. It splatted on the floor.

Shaune fell against a wall and covered her face with her hands. "I hate you!" Then she giggled a little and looked up at Meghan. "What kind of church members eat cake that looks like a severed hand?"

That's when the lights went out.

"Now what?" Meghan moaned.

Strange sounds, like hissing and dry leaves blowing in the wind filled the room. A great chill swept over them. Something scrabbled and skittered across the counter tops.

"We have to get out of here." Shaune bumped Meghan as she got to her feet. "I don't want coffee that bad. Do you?"

"Nope!" Meghan fumbled for her friend's hand, then held her free hand out in front of herself. Without even a hint of light to guide them, she found the wall and used it as a guide. Once they reached the top of the stairs, they were out of here. She didn't even care if she had to climb a mountain of snow or dig her way out. They were leaving.

The wall made a sharp turn. As Meghan slid her hand along, it bumped the stair rail. "We're at the stairs."

After what seemed like hours of stepping carefully, they reached the top.

"Where's the door?" hissed Shaune.

"It's gotta be right over here." Meghan shuffled across the floor to where she'd recalled the door being.

"What is that?" asked Shaune.

"What is what?"

"Look."

Meghan turned the way Shaune nudged her. Orange, yellow and red light wavered across the pews. Sunlight shone through the stained-glass windows, but they were no longer Biblical scenes. Now there were six panels. Four outer ones showed fire, the flames of which seemed to be alive; the glass appearing to flicker like a real blaze. Each of the two middle panels showed faces contorted in pain.

Meghan swallowed hard, locked her knees to remain on her feet. Shaune squeezed her hand, both of their palms slick with sweat. She turned. The door should have been –

A face appeared before them, lit up as though a flashlight was being held underneath it. It was the old man whom they'd met first. His hair still stood up in spikes only now it wasn't funny. They stared at each other for a moment.

Then he screamed.

His eyes bulged and his jaws unhinged, stretching his mouth open in an impossibly elongated 'O'. Hot breath swept across their faces, the shriek pierced their ears. The stink of death assaulted their nostrils.

With Shaune's cry competing with the old man's, Meghan ducked around him, running blind to find the way out. Suddenly the door burst open and in a great sweeping of wind and snow, the other man appeared holding the plate with the hand cake, a finger mark running across the back of it.

"Where are you going?" he asked. "You haven't had refreshments yet." He smiled. But now he had too many teeth, tiny and pointed. He offered the cake except now it *wasn't* cake. Blood ran from the wrist, pooling on the plate, running over and dripping to the floor.

Meghan's stomach churned. She swallowed hard. Pushing the plate toward his face she slipped past him, Shaune in tow. They reached the bottom of the porch stairs before they realized everything was wrong. It wasn't winter anymore.

Leafy trees swayed in a light summer breeze which brought the scent of roses and lilacs. Birds chirped, insects hummed in the bright sun. In the graveyard, someone mowed grass.

"We have to go back in," said Meghan.

Shaune shook her head. Her face was wet with tears. "No. Please, no."

"This is an illusion, Shaune, maybe a whole other dimension. We arrived here in the winter. The only way to fix it is to go back in."

"How do you know that, Meghan?"

A scream rose up in the air like a battle cry. Both girls turned toward the sound. Half a dozen children ran down the dirt road, puffs of dust rising up from under their feet. Each one of them wielded brightly coloured water guns.

Shaune uttered a little cry. "They're going to kill us!"

"With toys?" Leaving Shaune, Meghan went down the steps to meet the children. They arrived breathing hard. The leader of the gang held out her water gun. "Take this," she panted.

"What for?"

"It'll kill them."

"I don't understand."

The girl shoved a lime green gun into Meghan's hands, then took another from one of the boys. "Give this to your friend. They're both full. Spray the monsters with them. It'll kill them."

"Is it, like, holy water in there?" Meghan asked.

The girl shrugged. "I don't know. We get it from the stream that runs through the graveyard." She pointed. "But they don't stay dead long. So be careful."

Shaune had come up behind Meghan to take the offered gun. "How did you know we were here?" she asked.

"Mr. Heller is mowing. Whenever he mows, someone has come through the portal."

Another child stepped toward the women. "It's winter where you came from, isn't it?"

"How could you know that?" asked Shaune.

"No one ever comes through in the summer. But it's always summer here. I miss winter."

The other kids gasped and looked at the boy who'd spoken.

"Stop it, Melvin," said the leader girl.

"You don't miss winter," said Meghan with a laugh.

"Yes I do. Please." Melvin stepped closer and took Meghan's free hand. "Please take me with you."

"No," cried the other kids in unison and lunged toward their friend. "Stay here with us, Melvin!"

Suddenly a man appeared with a lawn mower in tow and wearing a tuque in spite of the heat. His shoes and pants were covered in a green spray. Mr. Heller. "Get away from there, you kids," he cried.

The kids screamed in terror and scattered. All except Melvin. He clung to Meghan as though his life depended on it. Scowling, Mr. Heller stomped towards them.

"Go, go, go," cried Melvin.

"Shoot him, Shaune," Meghan instructed.

Shaune raised her gun.

"No," said Melvin, "it won't work here. We have to go! In there." He tugged Meghan toward the church.

Mr. Heller started up the stairs, abandoning his lawn mower. None of this made any sense to Meghan. How did the kids know the water would kill them if it didn't work here? Why did this guy only mow the lawn when someone came through the portal? What portal?

Melvin screeched and reached for the door. As the man tried to grab the kid, Meghan moved between them. He grabbed her leg. At the same time Melvin yanked her toward the door, Shaune kicked the guy's shoulder. All three of them went back into the church.

"Is this the same one?" whispered Shaune, looking around.

The church was vacant and cold. Frost covered every surface. Melvin, dressed only in a t-shirt and shorts, shivered. Meghan took off her jacket and handed it to him. She'd be warm enough in the sweater she wore beneath.

The windows over top of the pews were now plain coloured glass. No depictions of anything.

"Uh-oh," said Melvin.

"What?" This from Shaune, panic tinging the word.

"This is not good," Melvin told them as the other man from before came out of the same room he had earlier.

Spying the child, he said, "Now, Melvin, you're not supposed to be here, are you?"

"You trapped us," Melvin accused.

"Oh," the man said, tilting his head in mock pity, "you don't like the place I arranged for you and your gang of brats?" He smiled. Meghan noted the tiny teeth. Then his chin dropped and the fetid scream came out. Meghan heard

Shaune speak, as if from underwater but ignored her. She had an idea that she hoped would work Steadying herself, she raised the toy gun and sprayed a stream of water into his mouth. He began to gag, the water freezing as it touched his tongue, his skin.

"Stop that right now!"

Meghan glanced toward the voice. It was old Spiky Hair Heller.

"Why don't you stay dead?" screamed Melvin.

"Shaune, shoot that one."

But the old man was wise to their tricks. He ducked Shaune's stream of water then batted the gun from her hand. Grabbing her around the waist, he threw her over his shoulder. She screamed and pounded his thin back with her fists, but he didn't notice through his thick coat.

"Let her go!" Melvin went after him but the old man opened the door and disappeared.

Meghan dropped the gun to her side. The first man lay on the floor, partially frozen, a large stream of ice sticking out of his mouth, looking like he'd choked on a giant icicle. It might have been humorous in another time and place. "Where'd he take her?" Meghan kept her eye on the downed man.

"I don't know. Probably the graveyard."

"Melvin, none of this makes any sense. Make it make sense to me and tell me how we can save her."

The boy sighed and parked himself in one of the pews. He shook his head. "No, it doesn't make sense and it never will. Look at me, how old do you think I am?"

With that, Meghan understood a little. Melvin was no kid. "You look about ten," she said. "I'm guessing you're older."

He nodded. "Twenty-seven. I was stuck on the other side of that portal since I was nine. Just because I was in the wrong place at the wrong time with my friends." He ran a hand through his short, dark hair. "Your friend isn't in any immediate danger. Not if she's smart. I can tell you the tale if you like."

"We have to save her first."

"Then let's go."

Outside, the blizzard had stopped but had dumped several inches of snow on top of the stuff that had already been there. Meghan's car was there, windows peeking out from beneath snow cover. Wind had scattered most of the snow from the church deck. The wooden posts were no longer carved but painted plain white. Meghan also noticed the angels were gone and had been replaced by empty, cracked flowerpots. She'd almost expected to see gargoyles sitting there. A few footprints decorated the snow on either side of the deck, but then they stopped.

"This isn't the right place."

"Yes it is," said Melvin softly. "It just keeps changing on this side." You up for this?" He nodded toward the snow they were going to have to struggle through.

"I have no choice."

"Technically you do."

"I'm not leaving her behind."

Wading through the snow to get to the graveyard was a long, laborious walk with several rest stops. Occasionally there were more footprints, but of bare feet, not boots. Meghan paused for breath beside one set. "Did he take his boots off? Why are these prints not consistent?"

"Mr. Heller is dead over here," said Melvin as if that explained everything.

Meghan groaned. "Oh God."

"He's good at playing a live person. Over this way." Melvin led her off to the right, between rows of gravestones just peeking above the snow.

"I can't believe this worked." Meghan held up the squirt gun. The water sloshed inside.

"We found out by accident. We also found out it doesn't work over there because the water can't freeze. And we could never get back into the church. That's why I was so desperate to go with you."

Meghan tried to sort all that out. None of that made sense. What was happening?

"Are you okay?" asked Melvin, stopping to look at her.

How much to tell him? "Not really. How okay do you think I could be wading through this much snow to save my best friend from a dead guy?"

Melvin nodded then continued on. Even though the names inscribed on the stones weren't visible, he seemed to know exactly what he was looking for.

"Here," he said, stopping suddenly. He began scraping snow away from a single stone. "Help me."

Meghan set down the lime green gun and started digging. As she did a bitterly cold wind swirled around them, blowing the snow, eliminating their progress. She shivered, wondering what the hell this was supposed to accomplish. Before she could ask, Melvin flopped in the snow. "I've missed this," he sighed, looking up at the sky, seeming to relish the chill on his face.

"What are you doing?" Anger flared in Meghan." We didn't struggle our way out into the middle of this godforsaken wasteland just so you could lay in the snow like a fool!"

"I have no idea what I'm doing."

"What?"

Melvin began to laugh. He kicked his feet and waved his arms like he was trying to make a snow angel.

"What the hell is wrong with you?"

Still on his back, he said, "Did you really believe all that?"

A chill worse than the wind and snow stole over Meghan. "All what?" she asked softly.

Melvin sat up. He smiled. His teeth were too small, and there were too many of them. Everything had been a lie! No wonder it didn't make sense.

Movement caught Meghan's eye. She looked around the graveyard. Snow swirling in the wind began to take on forms. Old Spiky Hair, the man with the icicle in his mouth, angels with bare feet and distorted faces, wings sweeping snow into icy spirals. So many more ethereal forms closed in on her as Melvin's laughter rang out.

Meghan tried to run, but there was no getting through the deep snow. When had this stopped being reality, she wondered. Was this a dream? Was she in her car? Where was Shaune?

Someone screamed and Meghan realized it was her. She fell into the snow, her outstretched hands plunging deep. Fingers so cold her flesh burned. She screamed again.

* * *

"Meghan? Hey, Meghan!"

Meghan blinked and looked around. A thick layer of snow covered everything, including a modest brick church, with a small brick porch housing its red-painted door. A tall brick bell tower, displaying the bell through open windows stood atop the back part. Although the church itself looked old, the porch and door, and part of the bell tower looked new.

Apple trees to its left wore heavy white coats that glinted in the sun, their gnarled branches drooping almost to the ground,

The dead-end road they were on had been plowed, barely, and the church lot not at all. Meghan recalled they'd passed a store/post office combo building. That lot had only partially been plowed. From somewhere distant, the sound of children's laughter whispered through the chill air. Had they passed any houses on the way in? She couldn't remember.

At the very end of the road was a small graveyard, a handful of black and grey stone tips peeking out of their white blanket. A battered, wrought iron sign proclaimed it to be 'Saint Peter's Cemetery'.

Shaune poked her. "Earth to Meghan."

Meghan looked at her friend, feeling like everything was in slow motion. Shaune frowned, a puzzled look on her face. Then Meghan returned her gaze to the church. The door was slightly ajar, an old man peering out at them, a grey tuque sitting on his head. No footprints led up the doorway.

"Did you hear me?" asked Shaune. "I said maybe that guy can help." She pointed toward the man.

"No. We're getting out of here."

"But—"

"I'm not wading through the snow, Shaune. We'll figure it out."

Suddenly an icy cold wind came up, blowing snow around them. A massive shiver wracked Meghan and she hurried back into her car on legs that threatened to drop her. In the seat, she glanced at the church again. The man was still there, but for some reason he'd pulled off his tuque and his hair spiked up to look like horns. *Old Spiky Hair. Mr. Heller.*

The shivers kept spiralling up and down Meghan's spine, forming knots in her stomach. Everything quivered. "Don't you remember anything," she asked as Shaune got back into car.

"What?"

Obviously not.

"What do you mean?" asked Shaune again.

"Never mind." Meghan turned the key in the ignition with a shaking hand. The car wouldn't start. "Dammit!" Yet another glance at the church revealed that the old man had come all the way out. "Shit!"

"Are you okay? You sound panicky. You never panic."

"We've got to get out of here, okay? We'll go get coffee." She tried the key again. This time the car roared to life.

Shaune grimaced. "I'm not really in the mood for coffee."

Meghan did a three-point turn, then, as they drove away, she looked into the rearview mirror. Three figures stood there watching them. Strangely, even as they drove away, Meghan could see minute details.

In the middle stood a ghostly figure, grey tuque in hand, hair standing up in tufted horns. To his right and left stood solid figures, one with too many tiny teeth gnawing on a chunk of ice. The other still wore her coat.

Behind them and off to one side, something lime green stuck out of the snow. None of them seemed to notice, but Meghan knew exactly what it was.

"Hey, wait a minute," said Shaune. "Where's your coat?"

White-knuckling the steering wheel, Meghan stepped on the gas.

Clockwise Dreams
Holly Day

Robots don't believe in ghosts, they attribute
the wheezing and clicking of late-night phantoms
to faulty streetlights and glitches on the power grid.
If a ghost were to present itself to a robot, the robot
would be able to dissect the apparition
as some clichéd space-time anomaly,
something broken in the universe
quickly mended by the natural order of the fabric
        of space mending itself.
There would be no need to haunt a world peopled by robots.

In a world run by machines,
ghosts would find themselves
completely explained or dismissed.
The shadows of what we were
would phantom hang or drown or stab ourselves
night after night, scream for an audience
that never feared or learned fear
but only calculates and classifies who an apparition
        belonged to
and why the ghost is a reappearing specter.
The grave sites will be kept up with meticulous detail,
flowers will be replaced, any new revelations
will be catalogued and stored and examined
in cold but sufficient detail.

The Spark
By Stephen C. Curro

Katrina grew up in a frigid world ruled by a tyrant. By day, she works as a mechanic. At night, she becomes the Ace, the King's personal assassin. She's not proud of her job, but she's accepted that it's the way things are. At least she has her boyfriend Dez and his little brother Uriah to light her life.

When Katrina is ordered to quash a rebel attack on the King's Command Center, she thinks it's just another job. But as she uncovers the plot, she is shocked to learn that Dez may be involved with the dissidents. Now Katrina must make an impossible choose— eliminate the one she loves, or defy the King she swore to serve.

The Spark is a sci-fi thriller about love, betrayal, and how the futures of others, even a whole civilization, can be determined through a single choice.

https://www.hiraethsffh.com/product-page/the-spark-by-stephen-c-curro

Subject: After Death
Debby Feo

What comes after
After you die
Child's query
Pondered by adults...

Happiness and sun
Relatives galore
No needs anymore

****

Going towards light
I am born again
Made to forget all
Previous lifetimes

****

Deja vu
Know you too
Wrong timeline

Whipped away
To another day
Hard reset

The Ascent of Old Cormac 'Round the Horn of the Moon
Lawrence Buentello

Cormac, an old man living in a small house on the shores of a great still lake, after having fallen asleep in his chair by a guttering fire, rose one evening and felt his heart drowning in sadness. In the shadows of the room, made strident by the dying fire, he spied the eidolons of his life drifting through the air like luminous accusations—their ghostly faces reflecting the ages he once knew, a child's smile, a young man's vibrancy, a mature man's desolated eyes, and now, the only visage living to join these lilting expressions, his own graying head. In a moment these visions dissipated into shadows and he realized his heart lay heavy for having lost the boy.

Gasping loudly, and using a cane to rise from his chair, the old man stood in the front room of his small house studying the air for additional fragments of spiritual visions, but when none manifested he strode through the front door and stood before the lake in the violet evening. Above him and the lake, mirrored by still waters, hovered the full sphere of the Moon, its white mountains and valleys shrouded by tendrils of alien clouds—its position in the sky directly above his house in the country.

This distant world had beckoned him from sleep, woke him from a dream of little Nalli, who must now be fully mature. Cormac stood watching the Moon ascend the firmament, ignoring the chill of the wind and the dew under his unshod feet, for he knew the boy had ascended to that world, leaving him alone in the house by the great still lake, having lived with him for many years before sensing the call of his lunar birthplace. Suddenly the old man realized tears were falling from his face onto the grass, onto his unshod feet, and all the memories of the years spent raising the child came into his thoughts and lingered; days spent fishing on the waters of the lake, lessons told and histories recalled, laughter shared in moments between daily chores. He'd loved the boy as his own child, though he'd never been married or known a family.

I must go to him, the old man decided, and the thought seemed so absolute no debate need be engaged, no objections raised—this decision had been made, and why not? Cormac was an old man, much nearer to death than life. He missed the boy so much his soul burned with sorrow—he knew the boy had decided correctly when he'd left his Earthly father, but the boy's absence left the old man without any regard for his own mortality.

Nalli, where are you within that world so far from me?

Determined, he turned away from the Moon when clouds obscured its face and wandered back into his house, but not to sleep.

Instead, Cormac filled his pockets with bread, salted meat, and the few silver coins he owned, quieted the embers in the hearth, and left his house, closing the front door for perhaps the final time. Then he walked into the night, his cane prodding the moist grass, along the path before the star-mirroring lake which led to the forest where dwelt the Gilidune.

Old Cormac knew he must ascend.

* * *

In the night the world assumed a supernatural countenance nodding toward the spiritual reality of its nature—and as he walked, Cormac spied the various terms of this reality, night birds flying to unknown destinations, their white eyes glowing and pale wings stroking back the invisible air, the burrowing insects ensconced in lairs causing the ground to tremble with their profoundly united shudders, reincarnated frogs risen from moist hollows singing symphonies more refined than any composed by mortal men—these natural displays might ordinarily keep the old man shuttered in his house awaiting the reassuring fire of the rising sun.

But tonight he walked with purpose onward toward the forest, ignoring the sibilant inquires of strangers on the path and avoiding, perhaps through mere fortune, the violent gestures of criminal hands. Shadows followed him along his journey, sometimes offering the reassuring shape of trees or boulders and sometimes bringing the wavering outrages of mysterious progenitors; and, at times, an eidolon appeared within a lingering mist, imploring him with ghostly arms to relieve it of its sins so it may transcend the chains of unpropitiated gods.

A pious man leaves the evening hours to phantasms, but Cormac endured their insults in order to leave the Earth before the Moon fell to the other side of the world.

When he at last came upon the rising sea of the pitchy forest he'd left many miles in his wake, and though weary his enthusiasm stoked at the sight of the tall, shadowed trees and he hurried toward the only path following freely through the close growth of endless oaks, maple, and ash.

But just as he stepped onto the earthen path, certain to meet his goal in the next hours, a figure emerged from a copse and approached him, though in the poor light of the heavy growth Cormac could only hear his utterance.

"To where are you bound, my friend?" said the voice of a mature man. "Surely not into these woods?"

Cormac paused, wondering if the man was a thief or brigand. Though prepared to defend his position, he knew he could do little against a younger and healthier man. Even so, he was not a man to suffer fools. He replied, "Is he who is asking this question truly my friend?"

Now the dark figure laughed, heartily. As Cormac watched, the man struck a long match against his boot, raising it to the meerschaum pipe he held in a corner of his mouth. As plumes of violet smoke rose into the trees the man's face became plain, and the old man immediately understood to whom he was speaking, for he wore the holster and vest of authority, within which hung a fine loaded pistol. Beneath the man's coarse leather hat a pair of keenly focused eyes assessed him, the halo of light from the match keeping both in comfortable illumination.

"I am the warden of this forest," the man said as the long match continued to burn. "Kernis, by name, and by my pledge I keep these woods bereft of trespassers. So I ask again, my elder friend, to where are you bound?"

Cormac hadn't expected to see the forest guarded so late into the night, possessing nothing but the truth to explain his presence. "I am Cormac, come from my house by the lake. And I must enter these woods."

"For what purpose? Are you a hunter or collector of mushrooms or succulents? Poaching is forbidden, and no one save by the magistrate's permission may forage in these woods. They are protected, as you must already know."

"I know they are protected," Cormac replied. "But I've not come to hunt or gather."

The long match finally consumed its fuel and left both men in darkness once again.

Kernis' voice echoed loudly in the void. "Then why have you come, Cormac? Surely not to be arrested by me?"

"No, good sir. But I must enter nonetheless."

The old man listened to the warden puff thoughtfully upon his pipe, the embers in its bowl flaring its light into the man's eyes.

Then the warden said, "I've been at my station many hours and only yearn for my bed and sleep. I don't wish to bring you to the jail so late, so answer now, Cormac, or be detained. Why do you seek entry into these woods?"

The old man sighed, seeing no other way but the truth. "I must find the nesting place of a Gilidune. I must ascend."

Kernis burst into laughter, exposing an ambivalence of character uncertain of its predilection for mirth or authoritarianism.

"Now I *know* you must wish to see my jail," the

warden said, his voice full of the humor of the proposition. "Trespassing is punishable by many weeks in confinement. But attempting to ascend is punishable by death. You must know this, good Cormac, so why do you propose such folly in my forest?"

"I beg you, Kernis, let me pass."

The warden struck another match, though not to light his pipe; instead he lowered the flame to his waist where his free hand rested on the grip of his pistol. "Tell me why you wish to pass, or tell me no more. You may either leave this path by your own volition or by my hand. Which will you have, my friend?"

Cormac lowered his head, knowing he couldn't give the warden any reason other than one that would conclude in his conviction for the worst crime known in his world. He said, tears in his voice, "I must ascend to see my son. He's gone to the world above us. I *must* go to him."

"You must be mad. How could your son ascend? And survive upon the other world? Explain yourself, Cormac."

"I'm not mad, nor has age abused my reason. It's a long story to tell, and not one clocked by matchsticks. Please."

Long after the second match sputtered to darkness the warden stood contemplating the old man's plea. At last, exposing a strange attitude for one imbued his powers, Kernis said, "Do you mean to say you lost your son?"

"Yes," Cormac replied.

"Then he is dead and flown to his next life."

"No. At least, I don't believe he's dead. He may be —I don't know. But I must find him, alive or dead."

When the warden lit a third match, in order to relight his pipe, his eyes held a more somber light, as if he kept secrets of his own.

"We will wait until my relief arrives," Kernis said. "Within the hour, surely. And then we'll adjourn to the tavern down the road where you'll tell me your long story that I may assess whether or not your purposes warrant the breaking of mortal laws. Otherwise, you may return to your house by the lake or find yourself confined. Which shall it be?"

Stolen away from the path to a reunion with his son, Cormac felt he had no choice but to appeal to the warden's good nature, which seemed hidden behind an ambiguous façade. He might leave and return the next night, but would undoubtedly encounter the same resistance; or he could try to infiltrate the forest in daylight hours, but surely he'd be seen and incarcerated.

Cormac accepted the warden's proposition, though he knew the story he must tell might just as well see him hanged.

* * *

When the warden's subordinate arrived, a young man bearing a thin face and a heavy leather coat, Kernis commanded him to vigilance, ignoring his curious stares at Cormac, and ushered the old man from the woods and back down the road.

After a half hour walk, during which they witnessed the rising parade of night-hunting owls fluttering musically overhead on their way to insulting the bodies of nocturnal rodents, the old man and the warden achieved the small edifice of the *Tavern of Many Woes*, long stewarded by the son of the original owner, a surly elder who'd killed as many wolves in his time as years he'd lived. Still, the lantern before the oaken door glowed warmly, as it had shone for nigh on fifty years, though Cormac had never trespassed its door until that night.

Within its dim interior, stationed strategically with benches and tables for those imbibing their cups, they settled in a corner of the establishment away from listening ears, though Egan, the current proprietor, leaned upon his counter curiously. The warden's slowly shaking head encouraged the man to quickly turn his attention to the bread crumbs fallen into his auburn beard.

When they were served, and Kernis drew a healthy draught from his cup, he studied the old man in the lantern's light sympathetically.

"Now tell me, old father," the warden said. "Why do you entertain mad notions of ascending?"

Cormac only stared at his cup of ale, unable to drink. His spotted hands seemed to him to belong to a man twice his age, for all the labor they had suffered during his long life by the lake.

The old man regarded the warden. "Do you have children of your own, Master Kernis?"

The light diminished in the warden's face. "I had a son. But he's been dead three years come fall."

"I'm sorry you lost your boy."

"It is a shadow on my soul. Why do you ask?"

"I ask because I hope that being a father, just as I was a father, would help you understand."

"Isn't your son also dead?"

"No. As I said before, he ascended to the world above us."

"Impossible, Cormac. Not only would the journey surely kill him, but if he *did* survive he would have immediately been put to death upon his arrival. Just as we put to death those who dare to come to our world from that Moon. It's the law of both worlds."

"He would not be put to death," the old man ventured, "if it was *from* that world he came."

The warden once again imbibed, setting down his cup with a clatter causing the tavern owner to turn his head. Once again the warden warned off his attention with a shake of his head.

"The things you have said to me," Kernis said quietly, "bespeak of forbidden acts. You do know your words are as good as a confession?"

"Yes, I do. I tell you this because I *must* ascend, but if you choose to hang me for my crimes then I'll at least have my yearning to rejoin my son mercifully silenced."

"It is good you understand the law. If I don't uphold the law, of what use am I?" The warden tapped a finger against the side of his cup thoughtfully. "And yet, I also have an obligation to be judicious in my estimation of the application of the law. Let me then reserve judgment until I've heard the full course of your tale."

Cormac pressed his hands to the silver beard upon his jowls, afraid, and yet compelled to unburden himself of a secret kept for far too many years.

"It must be forty years now," he said in a whisper. "I was a man in full vibrancy of age, easily keeping my house by the lake. I was a strong man, but of a solitary nature none found appealing enough for marriage, so I lived most of my life alone. But the lake fowl kept me company, and the stars always filled the water of the lake with celestial adornments. I would have continued living this way until my death, but one afternoon, after fishing the lake and carrying my catch along the trail, I heard a hue and cry from beyond the sedge and hurried to espy its source. I saw them running through the undergrowth, desperate, a family I believe, a father, mother, and two small children. It was the children, you see, that slowed their progress as they struggled to evade the crowd of men closely following.

"I felt shaken by the sight, for the people of that other world are unlike our own, with hairless heads and bodies, pearly, nearly translucent skin, long fingers, and eyes like amethyst, large and hypnotic. These four ran toward me, and like any man of the province I knew my duty, for who doesn't learn of the laws regarding the appearance of lunar travellers? But, having never been a violent man, where was I to find the impetus to strike down these beings?

"Before I might be required to act, a great riot of vigilantes exploded from the sedge and fell upon these travellers. Abashed, I knelt to hide in the undergrowth in order to avoid becoming part of their violence, and found within the aquatic camouflage of reeds and grasses a child fallen before me, having escaped the assault committed upon his family. A small child he was, too innocent to stoke illusions of murder in my heart, and terrified at having seen his family slaughtered by the righteous men of our province. A fleeting thought rose in my mind, to lift the boy into my arms to present him to these laughing men, but the sadness in his pearly face broke all ties to lessons learned of civic responsibility. I hid the boy with me in the grasses until the crowd had suffered death upon the others. Eventually, they tore their bodies from their gossamer clothes and carried them away on a cart bound for exhibitions in the village.

"Will you judge me for my cowardice? I only felt compassion for the boy, as odd as he appeared to my terrestrial eyes, and secreted him away to my house by the lake. Many years passed while I taught him to speak our tongue, while I dressed him in common clothes, learned which foods he could digest, painted his face with ores to disguise the pallor of his flesh. His beautiful eyes I hid behind dark spectacles, and never did we travel together to the village or seek the company of others. I'd previously lived alone, after all, and never suffered from my solitude. But now I had the child to raise, and made him my own son, teaching him to fish and cultivate our gardens, and also teaching him to sing the old songs. The lunar folk possess beautiful voices! He sang like an instrument plays, though over the years his songs became increasingly sorrowful, for he remembered his mother, father, and brother, and mourned their loss.

"When he became a mature man, or at least mature for a man of that other world, and I'd taught him all I knew, he fell into discontent and longed to be rejoined to his own world, which he remembered only fleetingly, as all children remember the past. Yes, he loved me, and called me his father, and so, too, loved our late nights upon the lake fishing in our boat until the sun threatened to bring the dawn and we hurried to our necessary isolation in our little house. But one day his yearning overwhelmed him, and he told me he must return to his world, to his people, for there he belonged. Why his family had descended to our world I never knew—were they explorers? Indifferent to the threat of annihilation? It's a mystery still. But now my beloved adopted son only wished to return, and wished me good life with a kiss upon my graying head.

"I knew I couldn't keep him on the Earth, not for my own selfish need of company, and so I accepted his pronouncement and escorted him to the forest where dwelled the migrating Gilidune. After he moved away from me in the darkness, I heard him speak foreign words to the shadows in a sing-song voice, and then in our own tongue he begged the creature to let him rest within its filaments. As I studied the black trees through tears, the unmistakable silhouette of a Gilidune rose into the night sky above the canopy and outward from this world toward the horn of the Moon. From that day to this one I've lived alone, until, on this night, I felt an unconquerable desire to be reunited with my son."

Cormac finally raised his cup and drank down all its ale. Then he said, "I committed a most grievous sin and violated many laws, first in harboring my son, and then assisting him in returning to his world. Master Kernis, would you judge me for the love that would not let me see him die?"

The warden had sat listening to Cormac's tale, his countenance never betraying his inmost thoughts. "I've seen the same man hanged three times," he said, "for multiple crimes committed. At the last his head fell from his body, but I'm certain he died at the first so the rest seemed purely ceremonial. Cormac, you have committed enough grievances to be hung on every day of the week."

"Then you will hang me?"

"I've told you of my own son's death, most tragically within the very woods I guard, as he tracked those illegally hunting venison. An accident, a misfired rifle. I understand your mourning more than you know, and I would sign a writ by the devil himself to be rejoined with my own beloved son. What can I say of your misadventures?"

"You could assist my cause, good Kernis."

"But you wish to follow your son upon the Gilidune, an act which will surely kill you. I should certify your confession and let justice be done. From this moment on, and in any way I could influence your future, you will surely die."

"But how do you *know* I will die if I ascend?"

"It's common knowledge."

"No one could know who didn't try. And it's forbidden to try, so how could anyone know for certain?"

"Appealing to my sense of logic is undoubtedly a wasted effort," the warden laughed. "I wouldn't be a reeve if I had good sense. But I'm not unsympathetic. What would you have me do?"

"Help a father find his son. If I should die upon the Gilidune, I will be just as dead as I would be hanging from a rope."

The warden nodded his agreement.

"If you'd known my son," Cormac said, "you would have seen that the lunar folk aren't evil. They are the same as us, Kernis. The old laws have too long kept us from knowing one another in kinship."

The warden sat quietly contemplating the breadth of Cormac's argument, his eyes glittering in the lamplight, perhaps weighing the manner of the old man's prosecution; or perhaps finding in the mirror image of the old man his own reflection of parental loss. Then his concentration broke, and he sighed heavily.

"I don't know if what you say is true," Kernis said, rising from his seat. "Perhaps one day new laws will be drafted. But for now let us break a standing law tonight. In any case, I'll be unburdened of your madness."

Smiling benignly in the lantern light, the warden led the old man from the tavern into the latter hours of the night.

* * *

When they reached the entrance to the forest again, the warden gestured toward his subordinate still guarding the path, muttering, "This man is my charge," as they passed; the younger man, obviously too intimidated by the warden's authority to object, merely stepped aside while he scratched his beard. Cormac nodded to the youth in parting, for the two might never see one another again.

Once within the dense growth of the trees, despite the clear sky and brilliant stars, the path lay desolate and dark. Only the warden's knowledge of the forest, for he boasted of knowing the disposition of every tree and shrub, kept the two from being lost within the shadows. Vibrant calls and whistles permeated the undergrowth, pulsed from the invisible throats of creatures whose temperaments remained untested, but perhaps, too, the denizens of these woods felt too intimidated by the warden to accost his company.

Deeper within the forest, Cormac felt the very spirits of the trees emanating from their branches, as if a faery mist swept through the environs; will-o-the-wisps darted brilliantly from time to time, offering signature to the spiritual nature of the plants and animals under the warden's protection, while glowing-eyed arboreal beasts flitted between the boughs, their phosphorescent coats shimmering with viridian accents.

The warden, a mere shadow to Cormac's eyes, instructed, "Stay close. We are entering hallowed ground and are subject to the poor manners of offended beasts."

The old man closed proximity with the warden, probing the ground with his cane for exposed roots, even as they moved off the path and wended their way through a subsidiary pathway which led down a slope and into a widening clearing.

Kernis stopped at the perimeter of this glade, his barely visible arm pointing toward a place farther into the opening. "Do you see that rising in the grass?"

Cormac peered studiously through the darkness, finally recognizing a rising mound like a small hill marring the smooth plane of the glade. "Is that the creature I seek?"

"That is a sleeping Gilidune," the warden replied. "A most magical creature, Cormac."

Most magical indeed, for the Gilidune remained one of the few mystical beasts capable of migrating from one world to the other and back again. Sentient and inscrutable, men speculated on the nature of its purposes for ascending from one world to the other, but no one knew for certain. Unafraid of men, the species of the Gilidune were inviolate because no man could harm one—possessed of a psychic sense, the Gilidune would vanish from men's sights if threatened, leaving an ill-favored mist in their wake fatal to living things. And so no men dared approach one of their numbers except for mischief, which was strictly forbidden by law.

Foolish men were legion, however, and therefore men such as the warden were required to keep the denizens of the forest, particularly the magical ones, free of molestation.

"I will speak to it," Cormac said, moving forward.

Kernis halted his progress with a hand. "Have a caution, my friend. You have no concept of its reaction to your request."

"We intend it no harm. Surely it will only listen."

"You're a brave man, Cormac. Perhaps foolish, too."

"I'm motivated by my grief, Kernis. Perhaps you understand."

The warden said nothing more as they proceeded into the grasses of the glade. The resting Gilidune did not react at their approach, but merely lay rising and falling in respiration. When Cormac stood only a few paces away, he cleared his throat and said, "May I speak with you?"

For a long moment both men waited in the darkness, but then a voice erupted into the air, not an *actual* voice, but one which appeared within their thoughts, as if spoken from the mind of the beast itself —

Why should one of your kind speak to one of mine?

Cormac paused, collecting his thoughts as he held his hands respectfully before himself. Then, "I have come to seek a favor of you."

The Gilidune undulated its massive body, and despite the lack of light Cormac could see the long, dense hair upon its corpus, longer than the height of a man, roll like a wave. *I give no favors to men.*

"Your kind have given favors before," the old man persisted. "You've brought those of the other world down to ours, have you not? Once, long ago, one of your kind brought my son to me from the world above us.

And his family, too, though they were regrettably killed."

Foolish of them to travel between worlds only to be killed. But why do you call a being from the other world your son?

"I adopted him when his family was slain. I called him my son and raised him. But when he grew mature he wished to return to the world of his birth, and so rode one of your brethren back to the Moon above these lands."

I know nothing of your son. But if he is gone, why do you seek a favor from me?

"My heart is breaking," Cormac said, truthfully. "I miss him, for he was the only family I ever knew, and I love him. I'm old, and will die soon, but not before I see my son again. I wish to ascend with you to the other world to seek my son."

The Gilidune's massive body shook again, and the warden stepped back a ways, perhaps in fear of falling within the beast's unhealthy mist. But Cormac held his ground.

You may as well be lying. You are up to mischief.

"If you could know my thoughts, great Gilidune," the old man said, "you would not doubt my sincerity."

Then let me know your thoughts. Unburden your mind to me, that I may see for myself.

Cormac stood waiting, uncertain of his part in the matter, but soon felt a strange oscillation within his thoughts, as if some energy were pervading his brain. Instead of fighting against the odd sensation, he relaxed and let the effect continue, for he hoarded no lies.

When the sensation passed, the Gilidune spoke again.

I have read your every thought, Cormac. I have your every memory. And you are sincere. I have felt your loss, your sadness, and understand your condition.

"Then you will take me above?"

Even sincere men court folly. You would die from such a journey.

"This is the advice I gave him," the warden interjected, though quietly.

"There must be a way," the old man said

imploringly. "You must *know* a way."

Yes, old Cormac, there is a way. Is there not always a way? But the warden is correct. You would die.

"You cannot safely transport me?"

Yes, that is possible, as you already know. Some have made this journey, only to die upon their arrival. I could take you into my filaments and keep you suspended in a magical vapor. You would not need to draw another breath until you arrived in the airs of that other world. But when those who dwell within that world aspy your presence, they will kill you.

"Do you know for certain?"

Are not all men alike?

"I may find one who knows mercy."

Unlikely. But I have felt the truth of your suffering, Cormac, and am sympathetic to your needs. You are a sincere, decent man among indecent men, and so I will grant you this favor, though it will surely assist your death.

"I'd rather die trying to see my son again than not try at all."

"When will you leave for that other world again?" the warden said, more sure of himself now; he moved forward to lay a bracing hand on Cormac's shoulder.

We leave now.

"So soon?" Kernis said.

The moods of my kind are our own. Climb upon my back, Cormac, and nestle deep within my filaments. The rest I shall accomplish of my own talents.

"Farewell, Kernis," the old man said to the warden. "I thank you for your mercy."

"I pray you see your son again," the warden said, grinning. "Just as I hope to see my own son one day."

Cormac abandoned his walking stick and slowly climbed up the incline of the Gilidune's immense back, struggling through the thick strands as if through gorse. When he felt as if he were centered on the creature's body, he lay expectantly, his hands clutching the roots of the filaments. In a moment a strange sensation pervaded his senses, as if he were intoxicated by strong drink; the field of stars above him glimmered like a host of fireflies, and now he felt as if he were in a dream.

In a moment, the massive body of the Gilidune rose from the glade and into the air as the warden watched amazed—the creature's massive shadow kept rising into the sky, along with its aged passenger, until nothing of the magical entity remained in the sight of terrestrial men.

Though he slept in a dream conjured by the Gilidune's magic, Cormac rose into the space between worlds, unaware of passing time, traveling through the cold of the ether as the beast glided unerringly 'round the horn of the Moon.

* * *

Cormac lay unaware of the amount of time which had passed on their journey; days or weeks or hours, he had no recollection of his own existence in that span, but when he came awake he felt his body still ensnared by the Gilidune's filaments, his mind still calmed by an unknown spell, though aware of their continuing motion through the heavens.

After a moment, he sensed the voice of the creature within his mind. *We have arrived in the orbit of that world above your own, Cormac.*

The old man opened his eyes but could only see the deep blackness of space between the dense filaments occasionally lit by brilliant white stars. He tried to speak then, but his voice seemed frozen in his throat, so he thought very clearly, hoping the enchanted beast could discern his words through other apparatus.

I see only stars.

I shall help you to see.

At once Cormac observed the stars within a black field flash between the creature's filaments as they passed, though he felt no turning in his own body—but soon the brilliant sphere of the Moon rotated over him to replace the moving stars, first the bone-white curve of its corpus and then the fantastic white mountain ranges and deep gray valleys of its geography. Because of the Gilidune's influence, the old man felt no abiding fear of the vision, only an appreciation for the awesome breadth of this new world.

Where shall I leave you in a world so wide and deep? Have you given any thought to your destination?

Cormac now understood the challenge of his task. If his son indeed survived on the world of his origin, where might he have gone in that world? The old man could search for years, until his death, and come no nearer to his son from where he levitated in that moment. If he weren't ensconced in the Gilidune's powers, frustrated tears would have come into his eyes.

He finally said, *Do you know where the people of this world live? Their towns and cities?*

The inhabitants of this world live in many places. A thousand cities encircle the breadth of these environs.

Then leave me near one of their cities. I will find a way to communicate with these people, I will let them know my desires and they will help me to find my son.

They will surely prosecute you as an intruder, Cormac.

I have come this far upon your back, blessed creature, so if that is to be my fate I cannot turn away from it. Leave me near one of their cities and I'll go on from that place.

As they descended toward the face of the Moon, and as this new world expanded in Cormac's perceptions, he knew his chances of finding his son were negligible. The enmity between the inhabitants of both worlds would never cultivate the sympathy necessary in the individuals he approached to assist him in his cause. But to die for that cause, which based itself in love, gave him motivation enough to try.

And then they alighted on the rough white soil of the Moon, raising a fine cloud of shimmering particles as the immense body of the Gilidune fell still. Cormac felt a trembling in his arms and legs as vitality returned to their sinews, then found himself able to stand within the creature's filaments unaffected by any enchantment. As he moved through the dense forest of strands and fell off the great body of the magical creature, he felt the exhilaration of a pioneer upon a foreign world, and yet he knew the thin air he now breathed might soon be stolen by unfriendly peoples.

Now capable of speaking, the old man said aloud, "Thank you, great Gilidune. I'll never be able to repay your kindness."

I've offered no kindness if my actions result in your death.

"I thank you nonetheless."

To assuage my sense of responsibility, Cormac, I will do yet more for you.

"What more can you do for me?"

I will give report among my kind of your presence on this world, and your intentions. Your name and circumstance will pass between my kind, so that one day your son might know you flew to this world to find him. But for you, Cormac, I can do no more.

"Again, I thank you. You've been a good friend to me, great Gilidune."

Cormac stood away from the immense and majestic creature as it slowly rose into the sky and vanished between the stars.

Now the old man turned his eyes from the stars to study the world which lay before him in all its foreign majesty.

And for the first time since finding his son, he sympathized with the impressions felt by the boy's family when they found themselves facing so alien an environment—for he, too, stood confronted by a landscape unlike any he'd explored upon his own world, white mountains rising jaggedly toward the lavender sky, wispy yellow clouds weaving through the firmament, and tall trees of azure leaves forming corridors along the light gray soil.

Beyond the trees rose the glassine towers and pearlescent domes of the people of the Moon, so toward these Cormac began walking, as he walked from the wilderness in which he lived toward his own village on so many days; though now he sought only anonymity among the wildly sculpted trees, bushes, and grasses preceding the lunar settlements. He realized that if he kept hidden from the people of this world long enough he might discover a method of disguising himself, just as he disguised his own son from detection—so he moved from copse to copse, obscured by tree trunks and the glimmering shrubs of silver nettle-like protuberances, observing the people as they passed, or from a distance as they moved from their artistically styled structures resembling an Earthly glassmaker's art.

In the evenings, he camped by one of the many small lakes surrounding the city, hidden by mats of grasses he wove, as luminescent insects floated around his head like rain-soaked garland. When he'd consumed the small provisions he carried in his pockets, he learned which fruits and nuts he could ingest without sickening, and, of course, the lake gave him sufficient water to drink. But though his surveiling remained undetected by the inhabitants, he knew he *must* increase the boldness of his observations and actually walk among the people.

Thus on one occasion, a tall, willowy inhabitant of the city, in the midst of loading supplies on a frame strapped to a strange beast of burden more reptilian than mammalian (though still bearing the doleful eyes of unappreciated toil), left several folded suits of clothes on a stump by the post to which the bizarre creature had been cinched; Cormac, risking exposure, though determined to advance his cause, flew from his hiding place in the trees to swiftly abscond with one of these suits before vanishing again into the wilderness.

Though the dull golden suit fit him imperfectly, the clothing completely disguised his alien stature, and to his great fortune the blouse also possessed a thin hood with which he could cover his human face almost completely. His hands he kept covered by the cuffs of sleeves far too long for his own arms, and though he still wore terrestrial shoes, he painted each in mud and soil and so the difference in appearance seemed negligible.

Emboldened by his new clothing, the old man began walking, albeit nervously, openly among the alien peoples, their hairless heads moving in uniform motion along the avenues, their pearly skin flashing in the sunlight, their amethyst eyes gleaming as they stared at his passing. But though he moved from east to west in the city, and then from north to south, he could not find his son; a thousand such cities must exist upon this other world, any one of which his son may have gone to, if he'd indeed survived his return journey to his place of birth.

So Cormac retreated to his lakeside resting place to sit in the tufted grass to contemplate his future, which must include moving from one city to another in search of his son, as long as his aging body would allow. The effort seemed hopeless, but still the only option left to him offering any hope. The old man sat among the alien trees surrounded by bone-white mountains, his sorrow limitless, his human eyes searching the sky for his own world so far away. But though his melancholy whispered intimations of failure in his thoughts, he knew he must continue to try to find his son.

But while he reclined in his reed-woven cocoon considering the long journey before him, a thatch panel of his hiding place suddenly lifted away, replaced by a vision of the open sky and the smooth face of one of the Moon inhabitants gazing sternly down upon him.

* * *

The old man suspected he'd been found by Kernis' otherworldly counterpart, a warden of the wilds of the Moon having discovered him camped among the trees, this caretaker immediately recognizing Cormac's Earthly nature and commanding him from his hiding place in the language of his own people, his forceful gestures interpreting foreign words.

Thereafter, the old man found himself imprisoned in a golden cage forged upon a sturdy cart pulled by two stout and brutish hooved beasts of the warden, animals which pulled him into the piazza of the city by a luxurious fountain occupied by water-issuing stone creatures of remarkable designs. While he waited so detained, occasionally attempting to speak in his own language to his captors, and with the few words he'd learned from the limited vocabulary of his son, the city's inhabitants paraded before him, their amethyst eyes shining wide as they studied him, their mouths agape in wonder to witness one of the legendary aliens of myth among their numbers.

These people didn't mistreat Cormac, but readily fed and watered him while he awaited, he suspected, for a high official to decide his fate now that he'd been captured. The lunar folk often spoke to one another as they stood before the old man's cage, and though he recognized contempt in many of their expressions, others gazed upon him with compassion, if not sadness; if only he could address that compassion with the story of his search for his adopted son, they might free him and assist him in his cause. But his fate wouldn't be decided by common folk of the city.

Instead, dignitaries dressed in formal uniforms arrived one morning and, after speaking sternly to the crowd, walked the beasts yoked to Cormac's cage into a procession of beings armed with long, curving blades and short rifles of indeterminate quality.

This train of soldiers and dignitaries, along with Cormac's cage, left the city and travelled down one of the roads until all present were kept prisoner by the multicolored trees and rocky terrain. Along their journey the old man marked the arrival of the familiar sun in the day, and then the astounding presence of the globe of his own blue world in the night sky, and though he tried to speak to the individuals marching beside his cage he only found a resolute stoicism in their regard for him. Cormac knew he lay in the conveyance driving him to his death, but though he felt no concern for his own mortality the thought of never seeing his son again filled him with grief. The old man wept in his cage, and no doubt the soldiers believed his grief only that of the condemned, but his heart broke at the thought of failing in his quest.

After many days, the train of soldiers and dignitaries approached a beautiful domed city of far greater majesty than the one they'd left behind, of a nature and structural grandiosity Cormac had never seen on his own world, and achieved entrance into this enormous bubble only after official recognition and approval. As they waited by the massive glassine doors, small flying creatures alighted on the golden bars of his cage, certainly not birds with which he was familiar, but featherless pink animals with large and translucent membranous wings. The old man extended his arm from above the bars and one of the flyers lighted on his hand, puffing a resonant song in the manner of birds, but much more melodious. Then the cart began moving again and the little flying creature lifted into the dark azure sky.

The procession continued deep into the heart of the glassine city as its curious inhabitants lined the roadway to observe Cormac's passing. Though the pathways and roads were lined with beautiful trees and floral accents, most of the terrain lay filled with exotic structures, towers, domes, and penthouses of granite-like stone, and stone resembling porphyry, bell towers ringing musically through the streets, and brilliant multihued lights flashing synchronously from sculpted metal poles.

But Cormac's examination of the wondrous architecture was only short-lived, for the procession continued on into a colossal, dense garden in the center of the city, passing vast orchards of exotic fruit-bearing trees and shimmering grasses, until they were met in a clearing by even more dignitaries. Behind these folk stood, to Cormac's eyes, a small cemetery, complete with triangular stones engraved with the symbols of a foreign language. But why should they bring him to a place of burials?

Still confused, Cormac watched the soldiers open the door of his cage and motion for him to finally step down onto the ground again, which he accomplished on tremulous legs; once brought before the dignitaries, one of their number, cloaked in a stone-encrusted cape and wearing a helmet crested with large feather-like plumage, as if to distinguish his authority, clasped Cormac's arm in his white gloved hand and walked with the old man until they stood among the headstones of the cemetery.

The dignitary turned Cormac to face a large inscribed stone before releasing him. As the old man watched, and as if issuing from the very ground, the misty impression of a phantasmal form slowly rose into the air and hovered above the cemetery. This phantasm's ghostly face formed the orbits of eyes, and then the rictus of a tortured mouth—

You have been brought before me that I may speak for you in this world, the spirit seemed to say.

The old man turned to ask a question of the tall dignitary, but the being only motioned for him to regard the apparition.

"I don't understand," Cormac said, turning again. "Who are you that you speak my language?"

What is your name? the spirit said sternly.

"I am Cormac."

It is good to know the name of a man before his soul is purged of his body. Cormac, I am one of among many of the men like you, born of that other world, who dared to travel to these lands against the laws of worlds. I was once mortal, as you are, but was tried for my crimes and executed by these people. Now I am detained by some special power of their people to remain in this world to serve as translator for all who commit a similar crime.

"How is that possible?"

Magic exists in this universe unknown to a mere mortal such as myself. I am in this world, which is all I know. Now, Cormac, tell me your story that I may relay it to these people. But be warned that no imploration will dissuade them from enacting the cruel penalties of their laws.

"Do these people possess no sympathy for others not of their kind?"

Do men of our world possess sympathy for the people of their world? Why would you give that which you never receive?

"Someone must give sympathy before this terrible cycle is abolished. Someone must choose love over hate."

Who will be first to do so? The peoples of both

worlds are afraid of losing all they give away. Now, Cormac, why have you come to die upon this world?

The old man, despite the apparition's dire pronouncements, inhaled deeply before telling the story of finding his son, of protecting his son from murderous men, and of his son's decision to return to the world of his birth. And of Cormac's wish to see his son once again before dying. He begged for the mercy of the dignitaries to let him find his son again, for only a brief reunion, even if they decided to execute him according to their laws.

"I love my son," Cormac said in a saddened voice to the spirit, "I only came to this world to see him again. They must have love in their hearts for those they care for in this world. Please tell them this."

Cormac waited in the cemetery as the imprisoned apparition relayed his words to the dignitaries in their own language, though by the expressions on the faces of these men he knew their sympathies weren't kindled. Once the apparition finished speaking, the tall dignitary turned to his colleagues and spoke, perhaps eloquently in his own language, and the others, listening closely, nodded their heads before bringing their hands together.

Then the dignitary spoke again to the spirit, and the spirit once again addressed the old man in familiar words.

They do not believe you speak the truth, Cormac. They believe you are only lying to save yourself from execution.

"I *am* telling the truth!" the old man said, raising his hands in supplication to the dignitaries. "Why would I come to this world if not to find my beloved son?"

I believe you, Cormac. But I am only the ghost of a man, and these beings are the ones who will decide your future. I am sorry.

The tall dignitary spoke again, and then the apparition translated.

You will be brought in your cage into the city center, Cormac, where its citizens will watch as you slowly starve to death.

The old man lowered his head, so very weary of his travails. "Why not simply execute me now? Why torture me in my sorrow?"

Your long dying will serve to discourage others from doing as you have done. This is their custom and their way. Thereafter, your spirit will be enjoined to this burial ground where your soul will remain until such time as they release you, or the very sphere of the universe finally shatters. My sympathies, Cormac.

Then the apparition returned as a fog within the ground, and the soldiers once again brought Cormac to his cage.

* * *

The officials of the realm didn't wish for the old man to die prematurely, so they gave him water every day that he may gradually succumb to his hunger. During the days, the inhabitants of the city visited the cage where he mournfully lay, blinking their brilliant eyes at his display, commenting sharply or shaking their heads sadly as their individual demeanors instructed their consciences; at first, Cormac tried speaking to these crowds, but they simply didn't comprehend his tongue, and so after several days he ceased speaking and merely lay returning their curious stares.

At night, after the inquisitive inhabitants left to their sleep, the old man lay staring up through the bars of his cage at the translucent dome above, which flushed clear after sundown to allow a brilliant exhibition of celestial objects to light the night sky. He didn't miss his home world, for he'd long lived alone away from other people even in his native lands—he only missed his son, who he knew he would never see again. As he lay beneath the stars he remembered all the times he and his son fished the lake, shared stories and laughter, gathered the plants and roots representing the boy's limited diet, always caring for one another in an uncaring world.

Cormac didn't understand the ways of the people of *either* world, their cruelty or their disdain for mercy. Perhaps his starving body also affected his mind and his thoughts were influenced by terribly unbalanced humors, but he found only madness in the lack of compassion he'd seen of the people of either land. Dying would release him of his physical pain, surely, but if these beings indeed interned his soul to their relics would his spirit survive forever in his grief? Would his soul never be free to fly amongst the stars in the firmament? Such an outcome seemed worse than death.

The days passed and the old man's strength continually waned until he could only manage to lie upon his side in the golden cage waiting for his body to finally fail. The dignitaries and inhabitants of the city seemed to sense his impending death also, for they gathered in great numbers now studying him for signs of lifelessness.

As he lay wondering if he could last another day, his eyes half-closed against the vision of the pearly faces, he thought he heard a familiar voice, as from a distance—or perhaps he lay suffering an hallucination—

"Father! Father!"

Cormac lifted his head to find the gathered Moon folk turning their own heads toward the shouting at their backs, and then a comingling of voices began murmuring excitedly—several of the attending dignitaries climbed down from the small dais on which they'd been standing to move nearer to the cage, though the crowd prevented their immediate progress. Instead, directly before the old man, the elegant inhabitants of the city began parting from the far edge of their numbers until the beings standing before him moved aside to allow a single Moon dweller to approach the door of the cage.

"Nalli!" Cormac cried, though in his weakened state his voice rose to no more than a whisper. He gasped for breath, but found enough strength to pull his thin body from where he lay to the cage's door where he could reach out to finally touch his son's hand again.

"Is it really you?" Cormac said, tears falling from his face. "Or are you a dying vision?"

"It's me, Father," his adopted son said, kneeling so he could press his cheek against the golden bars.

"I've come to you, I've come to take you home with me."

"How came you to me, my son?"

"The Gilidune, Father. One of their species brought the story of your arrival to its kind and eventually the Gilidune which returned me to this world learned of it. It flew to the place where it had left me long ago, and found me where I lived, and told me you'd come. Since I knew the temperament of the men who judge you, I begged the Gilidune to take me upon its back to where they kept you in this city, and it mercifully obliged. You shouldn't have come, father. Why did you travel so far?"

"To see you again before I die," Cormac said, smiling gratefully. "I *had* to come. I love you too much to die away from you."

"You'll not die, Father."

His son reached into the bag he carried and removed a flask from within. He handed the flask to Cormac between the bars and bade him drink. "This anodyne will give you strength."

As the old man accepted the flask into his hands, still warmed by the elation of finding his son, the dignitaries of the city finally breached the crowd and accosted Nalli with the assistance of soldiers. Cormac begged these dignitaries not to harm his son, but they ignored his pleas as their interrogation intensified.

The old man couldn't understand the meaning of their exchanges, but his son spoke forcefully, gesticulating toward Cormac, pointing to the heavens, and meeting every objection of the dignitaries with eloquent reprisals. The encircling crowds listened as if to a profound dramatic recital, enthralled; and finally, as his son cried passionately, all present fell silent as they regarded Cormac in his prison.

For a long while no one spoke; the dignitaries only gazed at one another, then to Nalli, then to Cormac, confronted at last with an exhibition of unselfish love between two worlds. Now they knew the old man had spoken the truth. As if confounded into silence, they meditated on these proceedings, then whispering amongst themselves, perhaps of the irresolute conviction of one of their own in opposition to unmerciful laws.

The chief dignitary then addressed Nalli formally, his words, though unknown to Cormac, spoken decisively.

Then, on the orders of the chief dignitary, a soldier moved forward to unlock the door of the cage.

Immediately, Cormac's son leaped into the cart and knelt to hold his father's white-haired head in his hands. Now his son gently fed him the potion from the flask, and Cormac felt a wonderful rush of vitality in his blood push aside the utter feebleness of his previous condition.

"What did you tell these people?" Cormac said between sips. "Why have they relented?"

As his son stroked Cormac's head, he said, "I told them you'd saved me from certain death on the world above. That you'd raised me and nurtured me and kept me from despair. If they were to kill you, they must kill me, too, for having broken the same laws."

"You shouldn't have said that!"

"Father, I told these men that I loved you above all others, above my home world, above all creation. They were astounded to know one of our people could love one of your people so deeply. I told them that for the sake of such love, they must amend their laws. No law must be held higher than the mercy and generosity of love."

Cormac laid his head upon his son's knee and closed his eyes. "What will happen to us now, my son?"

"They say they'll suspend judgment upon you until the greatest leaders of this world evaluate the implications of our circumstances. I'll convince them, Father."

The old man felt his son bend to kiss his head, and he knew he had arrived beyond the concerns of life and death; he now lay not in a golden cage of metal, but in the embrace of his beloved Nalli, and no inhabitant of any world could steal away his joy.

And when both Cormac and his son came before the leaders of the lunar world, a new era of understanding began, for the wisest of their numbers understood the bond between parent and child, and realized that love and mercy could be shared between the inhabitants of each world. After many years, therefore, the laws were changed between the generations, and travel between one world and the other became quite normal, as well as amity between peoples, and even the imprisoned souls within the alien cemetery were freed to continue their unfettered spiritual journeys.

    Cormac lived the rest of his days with his son joyfully in the mountains of the Moon, whereafter his soul flew freely among the stars after its transition into perfect filial love.

Taurus Season
Hillary Smith-Maddern

Last night, I became shattered pottery.
Hand pressed to your back, my mind ran
mazes. From behind vined walls,
I heard your shuffling feet, falling
leaves sighing. You are small corners of hope,
clear angles amidst jumbled pathways.
I have always been mesmerized by terrible
things. Like the way your voice strikes me alive
at each dead end of the labyrinth.

Can we pretend we are not both the minotaur?
Can we pretend we are not running for our lives?

The Oculist's Daughter
By Angel Favazza

The Oculist's Daughter by Angel Favazza is a steampunker in the old west. It's got a semi-mad scientist (her dad), her, of course, plus outlaws, Indians, Wyoming, a poison gas for killing natives, and an Indian guide. It all adds up to a rollicking adventure.

https://www.hiraethsffh.com/product-page/oculist-s-daughter-by-angel-favazza

Living Bad Dreams
By Denise Hatfield

When dreams come alive, there's no telling where they will lead. Everything changes when you realize that, dream or no dream, you're going to die. What do you do then?

Type: Novella
Audience: adults
Ordering Link:
Print Edition ($9.00):
https://www.hiraethsffh.com/product-page/living-bad-dreams-by-denise-hatfield-1

ePub edition ($2.99):
https://www.hiraethsffh.com/product-page/living-bad-dreams-by-denise-hatfield-2

A Place and a Thing
Holly Day

They send to the boy to the top of the mountain to think
        about what he has done.
It's just something that we do, this is what you do
when something needs to be fixed. There are boxes of birds
with their wings broken, eyes sunk into skulls
still covered with bright blue feathers
harbingers of spring, silenced. This silence is something
        to think about.

The boy sits on the mountaintop, hands figuratively bound,
thoughts metaphorically bound.
There are birds and flowers everywhere here, but they are
        not his to touch.
He can smell the flowers on the wind
the smell of wheatgrass baking in the sun, the
birds flopping in the undergrowth. They are not his to touch,
he's been told that they never were.
The world is full of souvenirs of conquest
but you can't get caught collecting them.

The Lotus Seller
S. Cameron David

"It's a nice day we're having, isn't it?"

You look up towards the sky. It's dark and foreboding, and you can practically taste the moisture in the air, mixed as it is with the scent of salt. His words make you grimace as you fight back a sneeze.

"Well," he says, holding out his hand. "I'm Mr. Jones."

"Really?" Something tells you that's not actually his name.

The man smiles, grim and sharkish, and wicked amusement dances across his face. "Well said, Mr. Winthrop, well said. But do you blame me for being discreet? Dealing with the merchandise we trade in, we want nothing too obvious drawing back towards the proper authorities. I hope that won't be a problem."

You shake your head and the man nods.

"I've read quite a bit about you," he goes on to say. "It's quite the tragedy, losing your wife and daughter like that. Fire's a sorrowful thing you know, but then again, it's not the first, nor the saddest sob story to come our way. You'll understand, only a certain kind of person would fit our clientele."

"But you can fix it." You bite out those words, trying to push the memories far from your mind. It's been a month now, and there never goes a day when you aren't beset by some paper-thin remnant of what you lost. The memories haunt your footsteps. Each day they come like the specter of a ghost, and sometimes you can dull them with a bottle but they're never gone for long. So yes, from the moment you heard those rumors—well, you suppose it's not too surprising that you would bring yourself to this. You close your eyes and shut out your darker thoughts. It's never been easy, but you won't need to endure this for too much longer.

Mr. Jones looks you in the eye and says, "I can't bring your family back, as I'm sure you're quite aware. Nasty story that was, and I'm sorry for your loss, but all we can do is mitigate the pain."

"But it'll be permanent."

"Yes," he says quietly, perhaps a bit bemused, and you get the distinct impression he's speaking to himself more than he is speaking to you. "Permanent. It certainly is at that."

"Good."

"So long as you're sure. There's no buyer's remorse where the lotus is concerned."

You don't answer him, but you suppose you don't need to, because very soon Mr. Jones is leading you away from the beach. Behind you, you can still hear the sound of the waves breaking on the shore. At last it starts to rain.

"Still, all the way from America. That's quite some distance, I have to say—makes me wonder how you found out about us in the first place."

"Money opens doors," is all you say, and he nods agreeably because it does.

And just like that, sooner than you expected, you come to your destination. The orchard stands atop a hill, each tree in bloom with sickly yellow fruit. They hang low off the branches, looking a bit like squashed up lemons. For a moment you think this is all a scam.

It better not be. Not after what you paid to get here.

Jones rips one of those fruits from off a branch. He looks at it for a long moment. "I suppose you know the story of the lotus."

"I know what it does."

Jones laughs. "Three thousand years ago, give or take a century or two, a king of Ithaca landed here. He'd just come back from a war—and I'm sure you know all this from school—and was trying to make it home. He and his men, starved and thirsting: they came right here to this very same grove we're standing in today." Jones tosses the fruit up above his head and, as he catches it, he has one last thing to say. "A warning: those who eat from the Lotus Tree belong to it forever. All your sorrows and pains will melt away, leaving only a dull and vacant contentment. Is that what you want?"

"Just give me the damn fruit," you snap.

Mr. Jones shrugs. "You're the buyer, I suppose." Then he tosses it your way. You catch the lotus, raise it to your lips and take your first bite. It tastes sweet, you think, as the juice dribbles down your chin, but already you can feel that blissful haze drawing over you. It's pleasant. Your thoughts are evaporating, slipping away from you like yesterday's dreams, and with them goes the trauma, the memory of your wife and daughter—what were their names again?

No matter. You doubt it's important. You take another bite, for life is good.

Pages of Waste
Holly Day

We gladly surrender literacy for the ease of voice
    control commands
images of food and treats on push-buttons, so easily,
    as though
there weren't thousands of years of written words and letters
    behind us
separating us from the apes of the steppes. You would think
that something so definitively human would be something
worth holding onto
but being able to press a button decorated with a picture
    of a cheeseburger
in order to get a cheeseburger
seems just as important in the immediate moment,
a wonder of technology.

There are those who will consider libraries a fire hazard as
    the temperatures rise
wonder why we're keeping so many books in one place
    in the face of global warning
suggest we fill the buildings with computers and puzzles
    instead.
This is the future of our legacy of literacy.
But I don't have to tell you that.
You won't even read this poem.

The Alchemist and Her House
Anj Baker

Time had passed, or something.

A summer storm had just ended--no longer a polluted, acidic rain, but a sweet, pre-Industrial one, one that the alchemist could never have known before the world ended.

Time had passed, but the number and order of years doesn't matter so much when you're at the end. Of course, the alchemist imagined (but she had never asked anyone, as there was no one to ask) that it would be different if you had children. Or at least another person, a flesh being who lived and aged like we're all supposed to, but she was alone and had been since the end began.

That rain had just stopped and the alchemist walked out of her little house and headed barefoot down to the garden. She wasn't sure where she was any more. She thought she had once been at her childhood home, deeded to her long ago, with pipes set into an eternal, underground spring, in a specific town in a specific county, but the more time went by, the more she felt like Baba Yaga, neither here nor there, in her half-alive house. She felt that she was somewhere very far and very secret, that her plants and books and the insects and chickens and the useless goat had come along with her into the nothing.

Once upon a time, she'd have had the equations to explain what she meant, but now she had only a few mangled words.

She called herself Jazz now, which is to say she seemed to have always called herself Jazz. She was sure she'd had many other names and titles and monikers, but she could not fathom what they had been, and so now she called herself Jazz. Mostly to say, "Damn it, Jazz," under her breath when a kitchen knife nabbed some skin. She had no one to talk to but herself and the voiceless beings around her so she was the only one who ever said her name aloud or otherwise.

Jazz never, ever walked past the horizon because she was afraid she'd fall off the edge. She was safe here, with her house. It had never seemed alive before, but now she had nothing left to do but imagine the realities where it was. She was Baba Yaga and she was safe and her house lived and breathed.

She lay down, prone, in her garden, a dead man's float among the cucumber flowers, her head set to the side, careful not to press down the greens. The slugs were out, and the worms, waiting out their peoples' apocalypses on little rocks. Jazz wished now more than ever that she had a dog, but if she had a dog, she'd have to find meat for it to eat, and she wasn't sure there was enough flesh left in the world.

* * *

That was the day the backpacker came, with their heavy, dark hair that shone red in the sunlight, a little too long to be practical or real, and their puke-green, virus-infected eyes. Jazz thought she was hallucinating, but the goat looked at what should be empty space and bumped his horns against the backpacker's leg.

She made the backpacker tea. Well, chamomile, as she'd long since drank all of her tea. They tried to gulp it but sputtered, having forgotten how to drink hot beverages. They looked at her apologetically.

"It's okay," said Jazz. The backpacker spoke a dialect close enough to hers that they could communicate.

"I should go," said the backpacker, and then, "You could come with me," at the same time Jazz said, "You could stay."

They stared at each other for a few seconds.
"You just met me," one of them said.
"So?" said the other.
They stared some more.
"It's nice here," said Jazz and she took the backpacker by the hand and led them through the house, room by room. "You saw the kitchen--here was a living room--nobody lives there anymore--" and it wasn't even a joke-- "--here's the bathroom--there's spring water and there's a septic tank--here's where I sleep and there's the spare bedroom."
"I should go."
"How long has it been since you saw another person?"
They frowned. "A while."

"Spend the night here at least."

"What happens if the spring runs dry?"

"The world would end before that would happen," she said, the response from her father when she had asked the same question, lifetimes ago.

The backpacker stared and the alchemist looked down. "I'll stay the night," they said, finally.

*   *   *

Dinner was potatoes and some greens and some beans and a poached egg each.

"I eat lots of eggs," said Jazz.

"What did you do," said the backpacker, "before the world ended?"

Jazz pretended to be nonchalant. "I was an alchemist."

"I didn't know there still were alchemists," said the backpacker.

"Oh there had been. It's not like I do it anymore," said Jazz. "What did you do?"

"I was a nurse. An ER nurse," they said, looking up and then down, to the right, remembering.

"That's an important job." A pause. And then whispered, "Was."

"Wouldn't it still be? If there were ERs?"

"If there were people."

"There are people."

"Name one!"

"Can name two. You. Me."

Jazz sighed, pushed her plate back a little--her plate of now-ageless china marked with holidays that no longer existed. "I'm gonna level with you," she said. "I wonder if you're a hallucination."

The backpacker smiled with half their mouth. "I know you're not. A hallucination."

"How not?"

The half-smile deepened, a dimple indenting their strained cheek. Jazz swallowed and wished she could just swallow her tongue. "Because you gave me dinner," said the backpacker. "I wouldn't hallucinate plain potatoes."

"I have to ration the salt," she said blandly.

"Of course you do," said the backpacker, standing up. They walked over to her, grabbed her by the elbow, pulled her up.

"Are you going to kill me," said Jazz.

"No," the backpacker said as they let her arm go. "It's dusk now. The lightning bugs are out."

"There aren't lightning bugs here," she said and looked out the kitchen window, with its flamingo print curtains, and there they were. Lightning bugs.

"Of course there are," said the backpacker. "Don't you know what latitude you're at?"

"I didn't think it mattered any more. There haven't been lightning bugs in..." and she trailed off and went to the kitchen door, opened it, and stepped foot on the patio.

The backpacker joined her, pulling off their socks and rolling up their pants rather than putting on their shoes. The pair walked down to the garden, and the backpacker followed her down the overgrown trail they had walked in on, the lightning bugs flitting around them.

"Where did you come from?" she asked.

"Where we all do," they said, smiling that sideways smile.

She smiled in spite of herself, and she wished the backpacker wasn't the only other person alive on the planet.

They'd reached the edge of the woods, the trail thorny from this point on, forbidding their soft feet entry. Maybe there was nothing beyond the bend in the path, nothing beyond the line of sight, lit by the tail end of the setting sun.

"Where did you come from?" she asked again.

This time, their smile strained and snapped. "I was somewhere and then I was here," they said. "I'd say how traveling works, but I don't know any more."

"What's that bit," she said, starting a trot back to the house, the backpacker on her heels, "from some novel? How riding on a plane is the opposite of travel?"

"I never read that book," they said, now even with her.

"Well, that's what it said. Because you go up and then you come down, and you've traveled while you didn't even notice, and so it's the opposite of traveling, and I read that and realized I'd always thought that."

"I never rode on a plane," said the backpacker.

"Oh," said Jazz.

"Never had reason. Or money. What's the goat's name?" Aforementioned goat was eating some nondescript weeds by the walls.

"Oh, I don't know. He's just a goat. 'Goat', I reckon," and they entered the house.

"You didn't lock the door," said the backpacker.

"Why would I?" smiled Jazz, and the backpacker smiled in spite of themself. "Water, or wine," she said.

"You have wine," said the backpacker.

"Not much," said Jazz. "But enough I can have some when people come over."

"Do people come over that often," asked the backpacker, the reticence in their face betraying the fact they knew the answer, the fact this wasn't a question.

Jazz's smile fell from her eyes but not quite her mouth. "You're the first."

She felt the unspoken question of, "In how long?" that the backpacker didn't ask, and ignored it, instead walking to the basement door, pulling it open, wending down the patchy stairs while the backpacker waited in the kitchen in the dusklight. She emerged a minute later, a bottle of wine in hand.

"Been a while," she said, and took a match to a kerosene lamp.

"How do you have kerosene?"

"Stockpiled it. Matches too. Don't use it, or the matches, that much. Only in this lamp here in the kitchen and only for a little bit each night. I'll show you the books in a second," and she pulled a wine corker from the drawer and opened the wine, pulled two enamel mugs from the cabinet, and filled each with a third of the bottle. "Follow me," she said, passing a mug to the backpacker and lighting a candle, her motions as lived in as an actor's, rehearsed, mindless, bodiless.

They were in the dusty living room, bent over before bookshelves, the candle casting misshapen light over the spines. The top shelves of the book cases held framed photographs, now blurry. She was afraid to think of who all those people had been.

"Who were those people?" said the backpacker.

Jazz said, "I think some are my parents but I'm not sure how many I had."

The backpacker said nothing and grabbed a book. "May I read this one?" they asked. "While I'm here?"

Jazz looked down at the floor. "Of course you can."

* * *

They read books at the kitchen table in the kerosene light for a couple hours, before Jazz turned off the gas flame and passed the candlestick to the backpacker. "Have a good night. You know where the bathroom is."

And she scrubbed her face at the kitchen sink and went in the dark to her bedroom. The goat entered through an inexplicable flap in the kitchen door and laid down in the corner, the shuddering candlelight turning his shadow into a devil. The backpacker swallowed and went to bed.

* * *

Days passed and they were all the same.

But eventually there came a night where the backpacker followed the alchemist to her bedroom. She didn't close the door, but took them by the hand and guided them up to her.

* * *

Early the next morning, the backpacker put on their shoes and wandered down the overgrown path, somehow already more overgrown--how many days <u>had</u> it been?--and made it as far as the woods before turning around. The alchemist--Jazz, she'd finally told them her name--would wake up soon.

* * *

Some time later, the backpacker grew sick. Radiation poisoning this side of an apocalypse, Jazz declared eventually, then kissed them on the forehead. It had been gradual, but now even their skin was failing them.

The backpacker nodded, a nod as pale as their pallid face. "Never realized how close I got to the radiation." They breathed out through their nose, and Jazz stroked their hair, pulling out a straggly, red-black clump.

* * *

When the house grew legs neither were surprised, but the backpacker left, saying, "I can walk myself." They made it as far as the edge of the field before they dropped to the ground. Jazz saw them go down from the kitchen window, but she didn't have time to go see before the house stood up.

* * *

The alchemist felt guilty, having her house walk everywhere while she paced her floors. She missed her garden, and the chickens. The goat was with her, but it was as if the backpacker had never been.

* * *

On a cold night, the house, half-alive, walked past a fire in the woods. "Please stop," she whispered to the floorboards, wondering how the foundation worked, where the legs came from, wishing nothing more than that everything was normal. That the backpacker was making egg drop soup. That their gentle apocalypse was fine.

The house stopped and crouched low enough that she could step out off the porch. In the corner of her eye, she thought she saw nerves sparking at the foundation.

"Hello?" she said, wishing she had shoes on.

"Hi?" said a person from a huddle by the flames. A dog poked a fuzzy head out. And then another. And another.

"You wanna come inside," she said more than asked.

"Sure," said the person and they and their three-headed dog put out the fire, gathered their bundle, and followed her onto the porch and into the house.

"I don't know how things work anymore," and she locked the door behind them all and flipped the unused light switch and the kitchen lit up yellow. The goat brayed and trotted into the dark safety of the living room and its bookcases and blurry photographs. The furniture swayed a little as the house stood back up and resumed a canter through the woods. "I really don't know how things work anymore."

And she showed the wanderer the bathroom and the guest room and the bookcases in the living room, the refrigerator that worked again and the basement stairway to nowhere, into the ambiguous foundations of a house that walked on chicken legs.

When the wanderer went to bed, the alchemist turned on the lamps in the living room and looked too closely at the photographs that were no longer blurry and she could not recognize a soul. She looked in the mirror in the bathroom and all she saw was a haze of green. She blamed a shower that had not been running, fog that wasn't there.

* * *

Since the house had stood up, the hot water in the shower felt pale and the yellow of the eternal lightbulbs felt jaundiced. There was always some vague food in the refrigerator, always salt by the stove, always a book she hadn't read on the shelf. But the water and the light made her feel sick, and she wished she'd died with the backpacker, out on the other side of the cornfield. She hoped coyotes had followed the backpacker somehow, lagging behind, by weeks or days or months, but following them nonetheless, and that they had eaten them. That the backpacker hadn't been left to the mold and worms and decomposition gases.

She feared she would never die in this house.

The three headed dog and the goat became friends, once the goat got over his newfound fear of electric lights.

* * *

She wasn't surprised, some days later, when the wanderer and the three-headed dog opened the basement door and walked down into the foundations of the house.

She was surprised when they returned, mere hours later, with flowers.

* * *

"What did you see?" she asked the wanderer that evening, her head in their lap, the pair on the couch in the living room. There was a TV now but they were both afraid to turn it on.

"In the basement?"

"Yeah, in the basement."

"I don't even remember," they said, and she believed them. "I already forgot. How long was I down there?"

"A few hours."

"Hmmmm," they said and gestured for her to move so they could stand up.

* * *

The wanderer was an endlessly antsy person. When they couldn't find a book on the shelf that seemed interesting enough, they'd pace the floor until a new one appeared. If a new one didn't appear, they'd go into the basement with the dog. Sometimes they'd pack a lunch for their meanderings. There was always enough food.

They were a useful house guest, faster at cleaning than the backpacker, but the alchemist wondered if at some point they'd stopped being a guest and now lived here.

* * *

One day, as the wanderer paced the floor, they looked up and discovered the string to the attic ladder. If the backpacker had ever seen it, they'd said nothing, but it was in the wanderer's nature to pull the string. And so they pulled the string and the ladder fell down and the alchemist followed them up, into what had been, in another life, an office and labspace. The walls were wood and the ceiling was angled and light patched through the lace curtains as the house trotted past sunbeams. The wanderer made a beeline up to a stack of papers, ignoring the dusty scientific glassware and equipment that lined the walls and covered the benches. The alembic still, the Tesla coil, the tabletop centrifuge. A strange assortment of things she could not recall having.

"What's this?" they asked.

"Old work notes."

"What were you?"

"An alchemist."

"Turning lead into gold?" They smiled.

"Something like that," and she swallowed. There shouldn't have been a lab in her house, not one like this. Not for her? She didn't work in labs like those?

The thought dissipated.

The wanderer left the notes alone and went to poke around the still. She picked the papers up herself, pretending to be musing, but trying to see what all they had seen. It was fine for the moment. They hadn't seen the worst of the work.

Eventually the wanderer tired of the office and descended the stairs, leaving her alone.

When they were gone, she looked down at a cell phone on the desk. It turned on as her fingers skated across the tabletop towards it. It unlocked by itself and she found herself dialing a number she did not know; it rang three times, and someone answered--a soft, androgynous voice.

"Hi! I'm dead," said the once-upon-a-time backpacker, giggling.

"Hi! I'm Jazz!" declared the alchemist, without thinking.

"The genre of music?" they said, an ancient joke, reiterated across three lifetimes. "You never did tell me what Jazz was short for."

"I don't remember it," she said, matter-of-fact, cool-as-a-cucumber. And started laughing hysterically.

The once-backpacker joined in and they laughed for a long time. It was a manic, relieved laughter--the kind that sets the listener on edge. The nervous and endless sort of laughter that betokened the conversation was far from over.

"Is this you? Is this really you?" said the alchemist, thinking in her head, yes, this is Jazz speaking.

The line was quiet for a second. "As far as I understand, yes. I do want to know how you got my phone number, though."

"I don't know--I just dialed it. What's it like being dead? Where are you?"

"One. It's not bad. Two. Purgatory. Which is to say, the old world. Or one like it."

"Back up, back up--" she said. "The old world?"

"Or one like it," said the once-backpacker.

"I don't understand."

"It's simple. The world never ended. It almost did. Or was going to. I don't know how we got here. There. I'd been gone a while. Don't know the deets. Had to have someone make a birth certificate for me."

"What?"

"I died and I woke up in a field, with the remains of a house like yours behind me and helicopters buzzing overhead. A hiker had reported a body."

"How did the world almost end?" she asked.

The line went silent. "You know how. You're in the history books. Your photograph. Jasmine Lee-Wheeler."

The alchemist was silent.

"Can I ask why?"

She took a breath and said, as carefully as she could, "Why what."

"Why weren't we enough? All of us?"

"I... I don't know. I never said that. I didn't say that. Right?"

"You did."

And they hung up.

* * *

That night, she stabbed the wanderer while they slept and they and the dog both disappeared. Blood never even made it onto the sheets.

* * *

She settled into a new rhythm. One where the attic and the basement were left alone, because they scared her. Two very different worlds--the old, sane one, but mixed up and repurposed and reassembled in a manner that had no analogue out in life, back in life, and then a new, primordial one, where flowers grew in labyrinthine basements, a world in which she dared not trespass. Her house was safe and liminal. She'd read books all day, the plots slipping from her mind as soon as she finished them--she didn't even know if these books had ever been real. She'd do the bare minimum of chores and eat the bare minimum of food, but it didn't really matter, because the house seemed to reset itself and she wasn't even sure if she could die.

Eventually, she heard a ringing from the attic. She let the thing ring and ring and ring and it wouldn't stop, so she climbed the pull-down ladder and answered the undying cell phone.

"Thanks for killing me. I have three dogs now," said the wanderer, not unkindly.

The alchemist hung up and hanged herself.

* * *

When Jasmine came to, she was on an empty street, being prodded by a peace officer. "Mx.?" said the peace officer, some young person.

"Sorry," she said. "Too much to drink, I guess."

The peace officer nodded and helped her up. And winked. And whispered, "It's okay. I know. We're used to it. Used to you all. You look familiar, though."

"I get that a lot," she said, and wished she'd grown her hair long enough to hide her face.

"Good luck," said the peace officer, and went away on their own business. A mercy, thought Jasmine, and found the ancient cell phone, now claiming to be on three percent battery, in her pocket. "No working SIM card," said the screen all of a sudden.

There was some bar down the street so she walked to it, her legs no longer used to walking on a real surface, but she made it inside.

"Can I use your phone?" she asked someone behind the bar. Their eyebrow shot up. "My cell phone's...been deactivated."

They nodded and gestured her around. She picked up the handset and dialed the last number that had called her.

"Hello? Who is this?" said the once-wanderer, picking up after a few rings.

"Me," she said. And then realized she'd never told the wanderer her name because she forgot it when the backpacker left. She said as much, but left out the part about the backpacker.

"I saw--I heard--when I made it back. What happened. What nearly happened. What you nearly did. They assumed you died."

"I guess I did."

"Well, you're here. Talking to me," they said. "Where are you?"

"A bar?" she said, and then quietly, "I forgot these existed."

"Me too," said the wanderer, smiling, it sounded. She *had* missed their voice, she found, missed the vibrations of their chest against hers. But they weren't hers anymore. "I'm hanging up now," said the once-wanderer, now a person. And they hung up.

She called the once-backpacker.

"Hello?" they said.

"It's me."

"I won't pretend to not know who you are, but I don't want to talk to you anymore."

"But I didn't know--"

"That's what everyone always says. I'll block your number if you call again."

"I'll trace your location."

A pause. "Touché." Another pause. "Some words of advice: this life is fine. Find a goat." And they hung up, and the woman named Jasmine, who had been an alchemist--no, no, a nuclear physicist--that's what her job was called--the woman named Jasmine, who had been a nuclear physicist three lifetimes ago, who had been spat out by each and every iteration of the world, stood still and listened to this version. The version full of human speech, pipes rumbling, glasses clinking, cars on the street, wind in the bushes. A world that had bumbled on, and still would, even with her in it.

The Lowing of the Stars at Night
Holly Day

The story goes that Cain was too selfish to sacrifice one
        of his oxen
and that was why he offered crops instead, built a byre of
apples and wheat sheaves
pumpkins and ears of corn. Or maybe it was some other
vegetable or fruit unknown to us
cultivated out of existence due to its phallic shape or
        unpleasant smell.

Perhaps closer to the truth is that Cain couldn't choose
        which oxen he could let go
having raised the lumbering brutes
from tiny, red-haired calves that gamboled at his approach
and followed him through his morning chores, to these mild-
        mannered oxen
too willing to put their neck in a yoke and pull a plow through
        the sun-baked earth.
Perhaps it was too much like the sacrifice faced
by children in 1970s Disney movies

who were tricked into offering their beloved dogs up for sale
or hand-raise a goose or a duck or a goat for their landlord's
        Christmas dinner
all because their parents had mismanaged the household
        finances somehow
burdening their children with a debt they were far too gentle,
        too human to pay.

Lasting Legacy
Lauren McBride

In hindsight, we should
not have been surprised
that they looked so much like
us, the aliens that teleported
down from their ship.

They arrived offering
goodwill and advanced
technology in an effort to be
friends, saying they wished
to be remembered by another
sentient species before
the last of their kind passed
away, their fertility rate
having dropped irreversibly.

They lingered on Earth,
visiting nearly every nation,
freely sharing knowledge
and healing the sick, creating
a legacy of benevolence.

Not until after their ship
departed did we discover
that leading fertility clinics
had been emptied of embryos -
the fertilized egg gone,
the future parents devastated.

In the end, the aliens *were*
remembered: cursed for all
time, infamous for their
treachery; their lasting legacy -
the Time of Weeping.

Slumber in the Garden
Mason Wageman

    I have never known the peace of sleep, nor the fantasy of a dream. When I want to rest in this world, my body visits another place. I called it The Garden when I was little because of its vivid and lush landscape, an array of convex terraforms drifting through the sky the way islands float in the sea. I named the hovering landmasses "mountains" because of their rigid shape, like diamonds made of stone and clay. They are miniscule in comparison to a planet, but the mountains in The Garden are boundless, like stars in the night sky. Some harbor entire cities, while others are occupied by lonely creatures who have only ever known their own species.

    Due to the chronic utterings of unfamiliar names and the rigid alien movements of my fingers, my parents worried that I had schizophrenia when I was seven. They gained the sense that my world was separate from theirs, that my body accepted reality in a different way, and they grew concerned. They attempted to label it with something medical, but the psychiatrist, Eleanor, could only describe me as a lucid dreamer. I found her description kinder than most, but it does not tell the full truth.

    "One time," I told Eleanor, "my friend Tulip and I climbed all the way to the top of a mountain! It took us for*ever*, and we were so tired that we went like this," I slumped back in my tiger chair and stuck my tongue out like a dead animal. It always chose the tiger chair because it had my favorite color.

    "Wow!" Eleanor grinned. She wore a cream sweater and a pair of perfectly round tortoise-shell glasses on her nose. She went back to her notes after showing me her big smile. "And do you remember how many hours it took you to reach the top?"

    I sat up in my chair and mirrored Eleanor's excitement. "I don't know." I threw my shoulders up to shrug, still smiling. My feet began kicking the air again, my heels bumping on the tiger chair.

"Can you guess for me, Mila?" she encouraged.

"Mmm," I hummed, "two hours." I bit my lip. "No, five!"

Eleanor's smile widened, and I could tell it was authentic. Sometimes I miss the way she listened when I talked about The Garden. She made me feel like she believed me.

When I am asleep in one world, I am awake in the other. Time works differently in The Garden, which I struggled to articulate to Eleanor. Though the landscape is extrasensory and far more vivid, I feel that the majority of my life has happened here, in the universe that harbors Earth. I describe our world as *The Heavy Place* to Tulip and the others that reside in The Garden.

The language in The Garden also escapes understanding to those here. Our bodies there possess the magic to create color and density in the lines we draw with our fingers, much like a tongue crafting unique sounds by rubbing the teeth and mouth. I explained this concept to Eleanor as "firework hands" due to the shapes' tendency to linger in the air, much like an echo.

It is strange to say that I was four years old when I met Tulip, as the other world is an ageless space where we drift through our lives like a leaf along a river, intimate with the surrounding water but unaware that it carries us forward.

I found her near a *teardrop tree*, where she sat with glowing blonde curls amongst a bounty of ripe fruit. From where she sat, she offered me a *teardrop fruit* with a chubby limb, and I accepted it with doe eyes. I held the gift like it had razors, but Tulip ate with such carnivorous passion that I decided to bite into the soft flesh, tasting music and whimsy with each bite.

"N a m e ?" I wrote with my finger in purple, once we had finished eating.

She tilted her head, staring at the shapes like they were alien.

The Land of Many Suns is generous, she said.

I stared at the image, entranced by her ability to draw. Her lines were smooth and flowing, infused with colors that lacked names. I attempted to copy her work.

The big stars shine hot, are the words that described what I drew.

Tulip giggled at my broken language. *I resemble a Tulip,* she said.

I breathed in her air for a moment longer, amazed both by her images and my ability to understand them.

I am Bird's Wing, I replied. My strokes felt weak in comparison to hers, my image sloppy and uncreative.

She offered me her warmest smile. *A Bird's Wing graces the petals of a Tulip,* she painted.

I jabbered on and on about Tulip to my parents, sharing my last adventure with her to the crystal waterfall, or the purple moon, or the underground city. I told them that we pet the fur of a *bearflower* together, or that we tasted the nectar from a *tackfly's* nest. It entertained them, at first. It was not the first time I had spoken to them of the Garden, but it was when they became suspicious that I was seeing things they weren't.

The imagination of children is so rich it was impossible for my parents to decipher how strongly I believed that Tulip was real. Sometimes, I would practice drawing shapes for her, though my fingers lack colorful filament in *The Heavy Place*. My muscles learned, as I knew they would, and my ability to communicate with Tulip grew as I continued to practice here.

My parents sent me to school before I began counseling with Eleanor. There is no education in The Garden besides the thorns on the flowers and the ache of a dry throat, so my schooling here would be my first. I find our education system to be the perfect allegory for our world—that is, laborious, goal-driven, and strict. There is a firm schedule, concise rules with direct consequences, and moral conflagration as soon as one escapes the enforcing eye. It was not a system I particularly appreciated.

Though my imaginative character drew the interest of the other children, they never felt comfortable enough to linger long in my presence. My offbeat ramblings and dissociative nature made my company unpleasant for them, as I rarely made eye contact or held a conversation of more than three words without talking to myself, whether it be with my fingers or my mouth. I was disinterested in *The Heavy Place* as a child, and when I learned that making a friend is not as simple as handing them fruit, I grew more apprehensive of my time here.

There was a boy named Kenny Nales who sat next to me on the swings sometimes. He was short with unkempt brown hair and a birthmark above his left eyebrow shaped like a distant bird in a painting. He was unafraid of trouble and an observable socialite with the other kids, but every so often he swung next to me on our shared chain pendulum without saying a word. He usually played tag with the other boys, but sometimes the adults forced them to separate during recess, and that was when Kenny was drawn to me.

"Why do you do that with your hands?" He asked. He tilted his neck to face me but continued pumping on his rubber seat.

"I'm practicing," I explained. I wasn't going half as high as Kenny due to the fact that I would let go of the chains to draw in the air.

Kenny pumped even higher, letting his body float for a second before falling back onto the rubber seat of the swing. "For what?"

"So I can talk to Tulip," my tone grew impatient, as he was distracting me from my training.

"Who's Tulip?"

"My friend," I said with a note of pride. I held the chains then, my motions stopped. "She doesn't live here."

"Oh," Kenny said. His chains rattled as he pushed them to their limits. When I was sure he would fly off, he slowed down again, closer to my speed. His eyes met mine, and there was a danger to them, something sharp that I did not wish to touch.

"Where does she live then?"

I turned away, shy suddenly. "The Garden," I muttered.

"Like at your house?" His neck craned even more; he was leaning closer to me from his swing.

"No! The Garden is just what I call it."

"Call what?"

No one had ever tried to understand as hard as Kenny did. "The place I go when I'm asleep."

He snorted, then he burst with sharp laughter. "You're crazy!" he cackled.

I dragged my feet on the wood chips to pull my body to a stop, then I darted from the swings, tears thick in my eyes.

The worst part was that Kenny went off and told the other boys, who lacked no initiative in pestering me about my secret.

"Where's Tulip?" they began to mock. "Going off to the garden today?"

Eventually, the teasing grew so severe and my crying so frequent that the teachers forced the boys to stop, and they did. It didn't matter, though. I decided that I would never tell anyone in *The Heavy Place* about Tulip again, and I didn't, until Eleanor.

Your hair grows, I once told Tulip. We lay in the center of a lake so shallow that it could not fully submerge our bodies, which were taller and more supple than when we first met. The lake sat on a pancake of a mountain, perfectly flat and deceptively expansive. Atop its flat surface sat a puddle of water that stretched for miles, never deeper than the ankle. Above the lake where we lay, a jagged mountain provided shade from the highest stars, and from the sharpest crag of its underside, a single drop of water slipped from its moss every few minutes and stirred the wide, shallow lake. Tulip and I found the exact location where the water fell, and we rested on either side of it so that the droplet struck between us.

My hair moves only with the wind, she replied.

I scrunched my brows, sensing that she had not understood. *Tulip stands taller than before.*

She shook her head, her blonde curls swirling in the water. *I am as tall as I am.*

I flicked my fingers in the water, splashing her bare body with the crystalline water. She gasped, hanging her mouth before sending a fistful of wetness my way. She giggled fiercely, but I made pitiful expressions with my face, streaked with water. Tulip turned to me so that her cheek was in the lake, her laughter quickly fading.

Is the Bird's Wing broken? She asked. Her eyes were the color of the lake.

My drawings crumble when you look at them, I said.

Tulip pulled her lips in her mouth. *You draw scribbles, and that is why they crumble.*

I sighed, focusing on the mountain above us, at the roots protruding from its underbelly, at the edges of rock, and the wet dirt that held it all together. It looked as though it might shatter if I touched its bare body.

My drawings hail from The Heavy Place, I said. Tulip did not respond, as she often grew frustrated when I attempted to explain the other world. Instead we waited, with our arms crossed over our naked bellies, for the next droplet to stir the space between us.

Around the time I was twelve, I began to lie to Eleanor. My first lie was crafted completely from curiosity, but its impact was far greater than I expected.

"I didn't visit The Garden last night," I said. I no longer sat in the animal chairs, but I slouched on an exercise ball slightly smaller than Eleanor's instead. Her office, a room with colorful rugs, scattered toys, and of course, the animal chairs, felt more clinical than it used to, if not fabricated. Eleanor was as bright and jumpy as ever, but I began to wonder if the exercise ball was part of the show too.

"By didn't visit, you mean..." she gestured with her pen for me to finish her sentence.

"I just fell asleep, then I woke up. I didn't see the mountains, or Tulip, or anything." It was my first time telling a lie of that caliber, and my forehead became slippery, my cheeks flushed.

I had ceased sharing about The Garden to any of my classmates in the three schools I had since attended, and I only told my parents about it when they asked. Their patience with my "condition" had grown since I was younger because I was far less vocal about the other world, and I learned to only practice my hand-speak in private. As far as they were concerned, I had essentially grown out of it; the only thing preventing me from telling them that I no longer "dreamed" about The Garden was that I knew they would take me away from Eleanor, who I was not ready to let go of.

"Interesting." I expected her to write furiously on her pad, but she bit the end cap and stared at the space behind me instead. "Tell me what you did before you went to sleep."

"It was pretty normal," I shrugged. "I brushed my teeth, and I changed into my pajamas, then I read four pages of my book."

"What book?" she tried, still nibbling on her pen.

"Dragons At Dawn." I tried not to smile as I realized I was getting away with it.

Eleanor made a "hm" noise, then she finally wrote something on her clipboard. "Is this the first time this has happened?"

"Yes," I said.

A smile curved at her lips, and she leaned towards me. "How did it feel, not visiting? Was it strange? Natural? Uncomfortable?"

I bounced uneasily on the exercise ball. "It was..." I began to sweat, worried she was investigating my lie, "strange. I'm afraid to go to sleep again tonight."

Eleanor gave a sympathetic nod. "Yes, I imagine it's a drastic change." She made another note on her clipboard. "Has it changed how you think of The Garden?"

I scrunched my brows, honestly confused by her question. "What do you mean?"

"Does it... feel any less real?"

I knew that Eleanor was only asking questions, but I sealed my lips out of resentment. She had never hinted that what I experienced in The Garden wasn't real.

"I'm just trying to understand, Mila. I know the Garden is very real to you."

Very real *to you*. It was in the details of her language that I figured out what she really believed, small phrases that were easily missed when I was younger.

"Yes," I grunted, my lips in a deep frown.

"Yes... what?"

"Yes, it feels less real," I said.

She considered me for a second. "Are you sure you feel this way? I'm not looking for a specific answer, Mila."

I forced my lips to un-frown. "I'm sure."

Slowly, I lost interest in speaking to Eleanor. I grew reckless with my fallacies, claiming the next week that I had not visited The Garden at all since I last spoke to her. I had been attending her sessions for five years, and she recognized my strange demeanor immediately. From there, she deduced that I was attempting to escape her counsel. She warned my parents that I was lying to her, but they sided with me, believing that I had "grown out of it," as they'd always hoped. They continued to send me to her sessions in the following months, concerned that I might "relapse" and fall back into my "lucid dreaming" habits, but I made sure not to give Eleanor anything. She grew impatient with me, and our sessions shortened, though she still gave me M&Ms. It was a few weeks before my thirteenth birthday when she released me. She had never considered me mentally ill, nor did she ever prescribe any medicine to treat my "condition," despite pressure from my parents. She was a curious scientist with an unusually large heart, and I still miss her sometimes. There are many stories I wish to tell her, secrets from the other world that would fascinate her.

I never told her that our bodies there lack reproductive organs in The Garden, but we produce more hair to carry a substance that resembles pollen. I only learned this recently as, almost a year ago, I witnessed my first birth.

The child was Tulip's, in a sense. Across many mountains and open spaces, she was the one that carried the dense pollen to the flower. *Starflowers,* I call them, as their petals form a structure reminiscent of the flare of distant light. They're voluminous organisms, with bright orange heads as broad as human shoulders and stems as thick as flagpoles, but delicate in consistency— easily cut and wounded, easily bullied by the wind. They are rare in The Garden, as they only grow where a human body has perished.

Tulip found the patch where a small pond was guarded by a cliff overhang far above. We were halfway up a mountain, a vast one that would take days of exploration, when she found them, a family of four. Their petals were velvet, the heads orange like fire. Tulip gently grabbed behind one of the heads and rubbed the *starflower* to her pollen-stained skin like a sponge. She giggled as she did it, almost as if the flower were tickling her.

It had been almost a year, a timespan that felt like days in The Garden, when we returned to the patch of *starflowers* on the same stoic mountain that hovered in the sky, independent and proud. Tulip and I sat on the scrambling roots of a nearby tree, ancient and tall, as we watched the pregnant flower. It was no longer star-shaped like its three relatives, but ovular and top-heavy, like a lightbulb balancing on a piece of copper wire. Tulip and I stared, entirely entranced as the flower began to bob. Its velvet head dipped a few inches, almost like an infant nodding off, then it dipped again, and again, deeper with each nod. Finally, the bulb dropped so far that its petals graced the ground, and in a globe of ooze, the *starflower* birthed a child into the grass at the edge of the pond. The child did not cry or wail, but they wiggled in their own slime, then they stood with trembling legs and began to stumble about.

Tulip pulled me behind a tree as we observed the child splashing in the pond with squeals of joy. They kicked and smashed at the water, liberated in the freedom of their own loose skin.

Tulip's smile was so great and unending that I thought she was a child again, and it occurred to me that she probably still was, and always would be. I felt tears arise, and I rubbed my friend's shoulder as she admired The Garden's creation.

It is discouraged to nurture children in the other world, as they are born with the necessary muscles and instincts to survive, and it is a rite of passage for our kind to discover another human on their own. Still, I understood the cruelties of nature, and I feared for the child as I heard their joyful cries. Tulip sensed this, and gave me an affectionate squeeze.

The Heavy Place weighs on you, she said. It was something she frequently repeated. I decided to let her words comfort me.

I decided in high school that I would make friends in *The Heavy Place*. I chose volleyball as my social hub, partially because I was tall, but also because it was the sport that all the girls played. I had estranged myself from everyone for so long, and I thirsted for normalcy.

It worked, at first. I played on the Junior Varsity A team, which was considered prestigious for a freshman, but I cared little about my placement. I rarely touched the court during matches, and a lot of the other girls avoided me because they were in higher grades. Still, we huddled together and cheered together and hugged each other after our matches. I was just thankful to be around them.

Ellie and Regina were the only other freshmen on the team, so we formed our own pack. We had a group chat with only us three, and we did homework together sometimes, often at Regina's because her family owned a gargantuan, pillared house. Sometimes my friends would tease each other about boys then turn to me when their jokes on each other were expended.

"So who do you like, Mila?" Ellie prodded. They were sitting cross-legged on Regina's generous basement couch, pillows in their laps.

I raised my brows. "No one," I said, avoiding their eyes.

"Oh come on," Regina moaned. "Everybody likes *someone*."

I panicked. They were already suspecting that I was different, then they would realize I was partially from another world, or worse, they thought that I only *believed* I was from another world, and they would laugh and laugh and laugh and tell the coach, and he would kick me off the team.

"William," I blurted.

Both of my friends gasped, mocking a vacuum cleaner. "Fitzgerald?" Regina pushed. "Or Shipton?"

"Um, neither," I said. "He goes to a different school." My panic eased, and I internally grinned at my own cleverness, but my face still reeked of fear.

"Oh," Ellie deflated. "Are you gonna ask him out?"

I shrugged, composing myself. "He probably doesn't like me."

Ellie's mouth hung open, ripe with drama. "He would

be stupid not to. You're gorgeous and talented and funny..." she hung on the last word to emphasize that there was more to say.

I blushed then, and began to smile.

"You know, Zeke asked me about you," Regina grinned.

I laughed. "Why?"

"Uh, duh! Because he thinks you're cute!"

"Oh." My smile had faded. I was ready for the conversation to end, to talk about anything except our bodies and boy's bodies and how much we wanted to touch each other. The truth was that I was beginning to stare at the other gender, to note the shape of their hair, or the protrusion of their collarbones. I hated that humanity was divided in half, and that we obeyed our genetic differences so ardently. I did not like that I was becoming a sexual being, and I found it strange how it seemed to excite everyone else my age. If this is what being normal was, I wanted no part of it.

I retired from friends for a while. I stopped playing volleyball, and I went silent in the group chat I shared with Ellie and Regina. The first time they gave me nasty looks in the hallway, I cried in the school's second-story bathrooms.

My parents' concern for me seemed to grow despite my insistence that The Garden had gone away. Every weekend, when they found me attempting to sleep at a strange hour they would ask me: "Are you having those dreams again?"

My insistence that I was not didn't deter them. It was true in a sense; The Garden wasn't a dream. My loneliness became another condition they needed to cure, and the more they pushed for me to make friends, the more I resisted. Instead I slept for ten hours every night, spending as much time in the other world as I possibly could. I felt much safer there.

I didn't connect with anyone from *The Heavy Place* until college, really. I attended a state school two hours away, as far as I could without sacrificing collegiate prestige.

In the confinement of cubicle dormitories, I found it easier to wave at people walking by, or to join the inappropriate card game in the common area, or to let myself be dragged by the wrist into a tiny room with a plastic disco ball and the aroma of weed.

My roommate, Cece, though not an enduring companion, was the one who helped me form all the friendships that lasted. She was tall with dark skin and wore long beaded braids in addition to adhering to an intensive, but rewarding skin-care routine. She had small teeth and a tight smile, and a giggle that caused boys to forget how to breathe.

Before we fell asleep on our concrete mattresses, she would fill me in on all the drama that day. "Jorge slept with Jason... One of my professors went off on this one girl in my chemistry lecture... Kevin texted me back, finally."

Cece found my quietness endearing, squealing "you're so cute," any time I whispered a one-word sentence in reply. She found it as a reason to trust me, as people of her energy often do, and soon I knew more about Cece than I ever knew about myself.

She was the one that introduced me to Amelie, my Tulip in *The Heavy Place*. Amelie was pale, short, cute, and at the time, only wore leather jackets and black pants outside her room. Her shirts often had floral patterns, and her hair short, brown, and impossibly soft, almost like it was floating around her head instead of attached to it.

"Do you believe in aliens?" was the first thing she ever asked me.

At first, I thought the world was playing tricks on me, like it knew exactly what I wanted and created a hologram to tease me. Amelie turned out to be the realest person I ever met.

We played chess and Minecraft and truth or dare if we were loopy; Amelie and I spent so much time in my room that Cece had to talk with me about boundaries, and I felt so terrible that Amelie never came to my room again; we went to hers instead. I had always been so far removed from other people's lives that it never occurred to me that Cece would need to make rules about company because I never thought I would have company. Despite my guilt, the incident made me realize how lucky I was to have Amelie, and I thanked the stars every time I laid eyes on their gaseous bodies.

"What's something no one knows about you?" she asked me one night. We were both sitting on my bed in the dark, staring at the jagged ceiling where faux constellations danced. We had bought a plastic projector at the thrift store that day and wanted to stargaze.

"When I go to sleep," I began, "I dream about the same place every night, and the same people. I believe it's real." The fake stars blinked at us, some faulty mechanism in the projector. "Sometimes, I think it's more real than my life here."

Amelie turned to me, her eyes like moons. "Every night? Like you've never *not* dreamed about it?"

"Never," I confirmed. "And it's more than a dream. I just say that so it makes sense to other people."

"Woah," she exhaled. "That's badass."

"You... you believe me?" I muttered.

Her moon eyes found me again, and she studied my face. "Why wouldn't I?"

It was also in my first year of college that my mother underwent back surgery and suffered chronic pain in the months following. Some days the pain clenched her body so tightly that she couldn't leave the couch, and I began to return home more often. I felt immense guilt for living so far away, and I found myself caring for her every weekend.

Between the demands of my classes and my mother, I began to sleep less, and I spent less time in The Garden. For the first time, Tulip and I began to distance ourselves from each other, going days at a time without making contact.

My companion in The Heavy Place experiences great pain, I explained to her, justifying my unusual sleep schedule. There is no word for "mother" in The Garden.

The Heavy Place clouds you, she said, her features sharp and resentful.

I walked away from her then, furious at her language, wounded by her lack of sympathy. In the time after, I ate *teardrop fruit* and hunted *tamborats* (a long, meaty creature similar to a rodent) on my own, leaping from mountain to mountain with a heavy tread.

Freshman year was also when my grandma died, a boisterous old woman who wouldn't let anyone leave her house without a full stomach and a plate of saran-wrapped food for the road. We had to bring my mom to the funeral in a wheelchair, and the microphone was on a lectern, so it was difficult to hear her eulogy. I cried heavily that day, and I felt sluggish and heavy whenever I transitioned to The Garden.

A beautiful leaf cascades down the waterfall, I said to Tulip. I was describing my grandmother; I was describing death.

Tulip reached over and painted her own lines to my drawing. *The waterfall leads to a new river, always.* She had connected the waterfall and river so that they formed a loop, an optical illusion that took advantage of the viewer's limited perspective.

I smiled, weakly. *It hurts to watch the leaves tumble down.*

She eyed me with concern, her long, curly hair fluttering behind her, then she rubbed my shoulder, knowing I was pained by a wound she would never see.

Amelie dragged me to a party one weekend, a Saturday where my mom convinced me to stay on campus, to be young for a little while. Reluctantly, I followed Amelie to a one-story brick house pulsing with yellow light. The hum of drunk college kids echoed down the street, and we snuck into the backyard through a broken fence gate. Amelie and I loved each other, but she was too curious of a person to stay glued to my side at a party, so I quickly found myself alone, nursing a bitter seltzer. I was already on my third. I observed my fellow escape artists, those who would rather change their brain chemistry than face another minute with a cold face, with curiosity. Then, a boy approached me.

"What's your story?" He asked. He was tall, wore a beanie, and looked like he played guitar.

I licked my teeth with closed lips. "I go to another world when I'm asleep." I lifted a lazy pointer finger to his face, widening my eyes as well. "I'm asleep in the other world right now."

He laughed. "That's fuckin' awesome."

In that moment, where a beer fire burned in a tiny metal pit, and where the city lights congested the brightness of the stars, and the air smelled of alcohol and sweat, I realized that I wasn't crazy. I could talk all I wanted about *tamborats* and floating mountains and endless lakes, and they could just laugh because they had another world too, something they could only ever describe to me, something I could never see.

"Sometimes I wish my only life was in The Garden," I whispered to Amelie one night. We were stargazing again, this time on a picnic blanket on someone's farm. We made the excursion after I heard that my grandma died. "Things make more sense there. They're simpler."

"Wouldn't you miss me?" Amelie smiled.

I giggled. "Of course. I wish our whole world was full of you, then I'd never leave." I was twirling my index finger through a strand of hair. "I just... wish I could float away whenever I'm here. I wish there were beautiful fruit trees everywhere, and I wish people made peace with each other, and I wish private land ownership didn't exist."

"You sound like a hippie," Amelie teased.

"I am a hippie." I continued twirling, and twirling. "I wish you knew what The Garden looked like. I wish Tulip could see this world and... see where my pain comes from."

I could feel the blanket ruffle where Amelie stuck out her hand. As I stared at the tiny suns of the night sky, I closed my eyes, and I pretended we were floating, adrift on a mountain born from a shattered planet, still rich with life, undying in its solitude. I slid my arm to the center of the blanket, and I allowed Amelie's hand to entangle mine.

Tulip grew bitter during our time apart. When I saw her, her blonde curls were duller, and her face more sunken. She chewed on the flesh of fruit with a lazy jaw, and her leaps between mountains were springless and dry.

I decided to address it the day we stood in the center of a field wild with red stalks and yellow grains, large husks at our feet from the *wildegrain* we had just consumed. The suns were as bright as ever, but our faces were greatly shadowed.

Your face darkens, I told her.

She frowned, avoiding my eyes. The expression looked unnatural on her, as if it wasn't a part of her programming. *A broken Bird's Wing suffocates a gentle Tulip,* she said.

I squinted with disdainful concern. *My burdens were bestowed to me.*

Tulip huffed. Usually she was never vocal. *Your burdens become mine when you cannot carry them.*

I stood awestruck for a moment, unsure of how to proceed, unaware that a single image could uproot my entire existence. The wind howled through the field around us.

They have become too heavy for my body, she finished.

I lifted my hand so that I drew an image directly in front of her eyes. *Your eyes have not seen half of my struggle.*

Morosely, she shook her head. *My eyes do not wish to.* We stood half our heights, staring at the other with great defeat in our eyes. For a minute, neither of us moved, not wishing to be the one that separated us forever.

Come to me when you have molted your feathers, Tulip said. Then, with her curtain of golden curls, she began to walk away, pushing the red stalks of the *wildegrain* aside to form her own path.

During summer break, I poured coffee for thirty-five hours a week, as disheartened and friendless as I had been in high school. I painted in my free time, attempting to imbue the scenes of civilized humanity with the wildness of art. Restaurants swallowed by vines, bedrooms saturated in pale greens and light pinks, sidewalks crafted from living wood. I sent pictures to Amelie, who adored them with explosive words. I never showed my work to my parents.

The Garden became obsessively lonely. With each new floating lake I dipped my toes in, and each new cliff wall that I climbed, I became convinced that I had never known Tulip, that I was the only soul to exist in the sandbox of floating earth. I avoided settlements, often crafted of shaved wood and blubbery *bearflower* leather. Though people are kind in the other world, I decided that I would rather die waiting for Tulip to return than join another in companionship.

When I returned to school in the fall, I felt empty. As an ecology major, I found our labs dull and unengaging, often subjecting us to predictable experiments with soil and worksheets asking vague questions. The only class I enjoyed that semester was Calculus because my professor told stories from when he served time in prison.

As for my social life, the vanity of newness had faded for those in my grade, and our once-open hearts were closed and frightened again, protected in their carefully crafted social bubbles. The friends Amelie and I had known dwindled, as people like Cece began to drift away. At first, I was perfectly content with the development. Amelie was the only person whose nearness I truly enjoyed, and I still preferred my alone time over anything. Amelie did not see the issue the same way, though.

"I feel like you don't make time for me," she told me one day.

I scrunched my face in confusion at the statement. From the time we had first met and then, we never changed the frequency in which we spent time together— once a week with the exception of the summer. Many people found that shamefully small for best friends, but to me, was exceptionally large.

"I didn't know you felt that way," was all I could say. It occurred to me only later that Amelie's other friends had been disappearing from her life, and that her lack of social encounters exacerbated her subjective lack of time with me. At the time, though, I could only understand it as entirely personal.

"I don't think I'm meant to be around people," I said quietly.

"That's not true," Amelie whispered. I wish I had trusted her words.

I began to wish that I had never known the peace of The Garden, that perhaps it weighed on my life here. Perhaps the other half of my life that had distracted me from the wonders of the real world, of civilization, of people who understood death and time and loss. I took melanin before I went to sleep. I journaled intensely about "the real world" and wrote at the end of every entry "The Garden is only a dream." I talked to my parents about finding Eleanor again, but they called her clinic only to discover that she was practicing in another state, so I tried another psychiatrist, and another, and one more. Despite every effort, I always awoke under a *teardrop tree* as soon as I slept, unable to escape my own body. I gave up on my antics, lying to my parents that the odd strategies succeeded, and that the "dreams" had disappeared again.

Then, I encountered Tulip for the first time since our argument, on the island where the puddle-lake stretched for miles. The mountain above it had shifted, replaced with open, sun-riddled sky, and the water's reflection was blinding. She was standing pensively at the edge of the lake, her toes half-wet. I approached her with a shy, quiet gait, gentle splashes giving me away. Tulip blinked to ensure I was real, then she embraced me, a gesture felt by every drop in the lake.

I offer medicine for the wounds I caused, she said, tears in her eyes.

No medicine is needed, I said. *I am content with a tulip at my nose.*

She embraced me again, her tears tickling my neck. She slid her arms on mine as we released, and she admired me with a damaged smile. *Your strength is greater than mine.*

My face stretched with a smile, my features difficult to control. *My strength is bestowed to me.*

Today, I long for sleep. I grow closer to myself with each push and pull of the solar system, finding love and appreciation in the many suns of The Garden, in the springs of my apartment's bed, in the sway of the *starflowers*, in the wicked laugh of Amelie, in the depths of Tulip's hair. I still hope I might find someone such as I, who eats and drinks and loves on the fringes of two worlds, who is thankful to find another human who understands even half of their being, but I accept the life in which I am the only one, the life where the greatest joys are only felt by first knowing the deepest sadness, and the most generous gifts only received by the heart that fathoms the cruelty of loss.

Apparently Most Serial Killers Are Virgos
Hillary Smith-Maddern

My friend, the Capricorn, claims this,
lips taut, a bow poised for passing prey.
Like his trivial knowledge makes him superior
to a month with a body count.

Virgos want to heal you, purify
your life in bleach until no blemishes remain.
We can make you better and we know
what's best for you because we see
the big picture, hear its technicolor.

Mutable signs seek synthesis
in contrast. It's what makes September
lustful for blood. How autumn tastes
like predictable change, hits the teeth like
burnt iron and waxes sentimental.
It makes a girl nostalgic for
hayrides & pumpkin lattes & graveyards
piled high with corpses who failed to follow our advice.

Who?

Kellee Kranendonk has spent a lifetime writing. According to her late grandfather she was born with a pen in one hand and paper in the other. She's certain that these days he would have claimed she was born clutching a laptop.

She's had numerous published pieces, has received honourable mentions, been short/long listed and she's been a spotlight author. Her work has appeared in several anthologies (more upcoming). Some of her pieces were to appear in a school book project, though that didn't pan out. For nine years, Kellee was the editor Youth Imagination and a children's magazine prior to that. She has also managed online writers' groups.

Kellee lives in a newly amalgamated Municipality in the Maritime province of New Brunswick, Canada.

Mason Wageman is a student at the University of Denver studying English and Computer Science. He also serves as an editor for Foothills, the school's literary and arts magazine, as well as The Clarion, the school's student newspaper.

Anj Baker holds a bachelor's degree in biology, and has also held many different jobs, from quality analysis to cheese-mongering to teaching chemistry. Baker lives, works, and writes melancholy speculative fiction in Lexington, Kentucky, USA, with two guinea pigs and a jungle of houseplants.

Hillary Smith-Maddern is a proud cat mom, once-excellent and now-solidly-mediocre bassoon player, and collector of dilapidated plants. Her favorite things include cats, coffee, cobblestone streets, and the crisp, blank pages of a writing notebook. She resides in Greenfield, MA and enjoys exploring the world. When she's not writing, you can find her coaching, hiking a mountain, or yelling about the patriarchy. Her poetry is an evocative exploration of some of life's most formative moments. She is the 2023 runner up for the Beals' Poetry Prize and some of her work has been featured in Only Poems, As It Ought to Be Magazine, Ghost City Review, Sheepshead Review, and Coneflower Cafe.

A longtime resident of New York State, **S. Cameron David** has had a fascination for mythology and fantasy for as long as he could remember. A former student of history, now he prefers living in his own invented worlds.

Lauren McBride finds inspiration in faith, family, nature, science, and membership in the SFPA. Nominated for the Best of the Net, Rhysling, and Dwarf Stars Awards, her poetry has appeared in dozens of publications including *Asimov's, Fantasy & Science Fiction,* and *Scifaikuest*. She enjoys swimming, gardening, baking, reading, writing, and knitting scarves for our troops.

Holly Day's poetry has recently appeared in *Slipstream, Penumbric,* and *Maintenant.* She is the co-author of the books, *Music Theory for Dummies* and *Music Composition for Dummies* and currently works as an instructor at The Richard Hugo Center in Seattle and at the Loft Literary Center in Minneapolis.

www.ingramcontent.com/pod-product-compliance
Lightning Source LLC
LaVergne TN
LVHW012031060526
838201LV00061B/4561